For Now

KCP Fiction is an imprint of Kids Can Press

Kids Can Press acknowledges the financial support of the Government of Ontario, through the Ontario Media Development Corporation's Ontario Book Initiative; the Ontario Arts Council; the Canada Council for the Arts; and the Government of Canada, through the BPIDP, for our publishing activity.

Published in Canada by
Kids Can Press Ltd.
29 Birch Avenue
Toronto, ON M4V 1E2

Published in the U.S. by
Kids Can Press Ltd.
2250 Military Road
Tonawanda, NY 14150

www.kidscanpress.com

Edited by Charis Wahl
Designed by Marie Bartholomew
Cover illustration by Marie Bartholomew
Printed and bound in Canada

CM 07 0 9 8 7 6 5 4 3 2 1
CM PA 07 0 9 8 7 6 5 4 3 2 1

Library and Archives Canada Cataloguing in Publication

Friesen, Gayle
For now / written by by Gayle Friesen.

ISBN-13: 978-1-55453-132-5 (bound)
ISBN-13: 978-1-55453-133-2 (pbk.)
ISBN-10: 1-55453-132-2 (bound)
ISBN-10: 1-55453-133-0 (pbk.)

I. Title.

PS8561.R4956F67 2007 jC813'.54 C2006-906851-8

Kids Can Press is a Corus™ Entertainment company

For Now

Gayle Friesen

KCP Fiction

To Susie, for now as well as then

Acknowledgments

The Joseph Campbell quotes can be found in *The Power of Myth* © 1988 by Apostrophe S Productions, Inc., and Alfred van der Marck Editions. Published by Doubleday (hardcover) and Anchor Books (paperback).

Thanks again to Charis and Jennifer for making the book better the way they do. A special thanks to Charis for finding the title. Always thanks to my writing readers: Christy and Alison.

Prologue

Once upon a time there was a beautiful princess. When she was very young she met a prince who was also very young (and who would be cuter when he got a better hairstyle). The prince and the princess married. In the royal wedding photo they looked like they were twelve years old. He wore a pale blue suit; I don't know how that happened. For a time they were ridiculously happy. He built her a house and painted the walls in crazy, psychedelic colors; and they had picnics in the middle of every room. They made a baby. (Probably during one of the picnics.) There was singing in the land and the sounding of trumpets when it was announced that the princess was with daughter. Portraits were made of the princess's burgeoning belly. The prince grew a moustache. A few years later there was another girl child. There was more singing and resounding of trumpet-song. Happiness reigned. But then the younger daughter died. She was young enough to know not much, old enough to bring a great sorrow upon the land. The princess and her prince grew sad. And apart. The princess sat in her castle weaving wispy, soft garments that would never be worn. The prince built furniture from wood that would never be used.

As time passed, the princess got busy with her job and the prince got busy with a lady-in-waiting. Eventually they fled to different parts of the kingdom and to different places in their hearts. The princess found another prince — more like an earl or a duke — and believed she could love him forever. She talked her remaining daughter into the idea. The remaining daughter was a darned good sport, if you ask me. The remaining daughter wanted to believe in love. Who doesn't want to believe in love?

Falltime

Chapter One

I thought I was through with fairy tales, but I found myself backsliding to the happy-ever-after place when my mom got married again. What can I say — it's like brown is the new black or green is the new pink. Second marriages are the new first. There was gauze and twinkly little white lights wrapped around tree trunks and really good cake. (Not just chocolate. There was also a white cake with chocolate icing and custard and something called ganache. Do I know what ganache is? No, not really, except that it's yummy.) I blame the ganache. And the fact that I danced with Sam. He seemed about to kiss me at one point until his little brother Danny started barfing from eating five pieces of cake and from being chased by his other brother Henry. (Expect to see Henry's face on a Most-Wanted TV show one day.) But mostly I backslided — or backslid, whatever — because I let myself. I thought I'd figured some things out: *change was inevitable; ergo, change was okay*. Not exactly quantum physics, but it was a leap for me.

So, these days, I'm feeling cautiously optimistic. I have a prospective boyfriend (Sam: boy next door, lifetime friend). I am back in my best friend Dell's good graces after a summertime feud (regarding ex-boyfriend, Marshall, and how I saw him making out with my prospective — now official — stepsister, Angela, in a cornfield and felt the need to report). My mom and new stepfather (Cal) have returned from the honeymoon and are still in love. (She had to make a point of letting me know, with overly arched eyebrows, that "the honeymoon went well. Really well, if you know what I mean." I knew what she meant.) What else? My dad started renovating houses, which is better than sitting around in his sad little apartment reading sad, gigantic Russian novels. Oh, and I grew two inches this summer so that means I'm almost five feet, three inches. Considerable by any standard, except maybe my new stepsister Angela's — who is tall and blond and beautiful, but I've decided not to hold this against her in keeping with my new optimism. That's about it, except that I started school a couple of days ago and have, consequently, found my true calling. That was a bonus, I have to admit.

I was a little nervous because I'm going to a bigger school and starting eleventh grade, which is a big deal due to the need to get good grades in order to get into a good college in order to have a good and productive life. (That little commercial was sponsored by my mother, who has been saying this for the last fifteen years.) I really have nothing against leading a good and productive life. Besides, even though my attitude has improved greatly toward Angela (whom, until quite recently, I knew only as a psychotic, shoplifting, boyfriend-stealing phony) I am realistic enough to know that since she is beautiful, I am going to have to be the smart one. Well, except that Angela is also smart ... and thin, and ... yeah, I'm definitely going to have to be the optimistic one.

Every once in a while I have a mental movie-montage of my life thus far. It starts with a mom and a dad, a me and a baby sister. Cut to an accident that takes baby sister away. Cut again to the divorce. Dad gets depressed; Mom gets a boyfriend. Mom gets engaged. New guy comes with über-beautiful daughter, Angela. Players struggle to shift their seats, make room for the new. Plot thickens. Freeze. The *me*-character (that's me, Jes) must decide whether to tell Dell about Über-Angela and creepy Marshall. It's a long freeze-frame because it's about telling the truth. *Me* decides to tell. *Me* is confused. *Me* doesn't know what happens next. *Me* decides that if she doesn't want to become extinct, like a dinosaur or dodo bird, *me* will need to evolve. End of montage.

So, I signed up for Psychology 101. I thought it might help. Also, I thought it would be an easy course because my mother is a therapist. I've picked up a bit of stuff over the years — mostly body language: involuntary grimaces, averted gazes, tense toes, that kind of thing. I figured it would be like taking French when your family is bilingual. But I had no idea, absolutely none, of the depth and breadth of what I would learn in this course. My teacher is very enthusiastic. If I am now a cautious optimist, I think it would be fair to say that Mr. Truelove is a *raging* optimist.

To tell you the truth, it's been a few years since I was really impressed with any of my teachers. There was Ms. Batty, who dressed up as a vampire every single Halloween, but that was in the third grade. And I liked Mr. Kwong for his soft-spoken ways as well as his napping ways during reading time. But, other than that, I've been short on inspiring adult role models. Watching your parents go through a divorce will do that to a person. Anyway, that's the old me. The new one is on the verge, I'm sure, of finding a mentor who will guide me along the path of optimism and hopefulness.

The guy is not much to look at, but that name — how can you ignore that name? Mr. Truelove. It's like Mr. Right, but so much more satisfying. Dell noticed his mismatched socks right away — not a surprising observation when you consider that she is an aspiring writer; but, still, I told her she was being superficial. He has that almost painful look of fervor that comes with new teachers the way fries come with a burger, where you just know they can't wait to rhapsodize about *following your bliss*. And he was wearing the corduroy blazer with the patches on the elbows that must come free with every teaching degree.

I admit I was skeptical at first, especially when he looked around the class making eye contact. Straight out of my mom's bag of tricks: *how to establish connection*. But then he opened his mouth and began to speak in a husky, sexy, deejay voice: "Should an introductory course in psychology lead you to a better understanding of human behavior and thus to improved insight into yourself and others?" He paused, established more eye contact and smiled. I waited, still skeptical. Anybody can make an opening statement, right? But then he bellowed, "By and large, yes!" and slammed the front desk with his hand, which unfortunately was the desk of Jumpy Kate, who then did what she does — jumped and squealed. He apologized and said, "I just get so excited."

This could have been the kiss of death for Mr. Truelove. In fact, it should have been. Troy and Flynn — notorious milk-money stealers in second grade, infamous guinea-pig terrorizers in fifth grade — leapt on the comment like cats on mice. They started saying stuff about Mr. Truelove "getting so excited." (As my mom would say, *if you know what I mean*.)

Mr. Truelove walked to the back of the room, opened the door and, with a courtly gesture, told them to go visit the principal, Ms. Blanchard. Flynn sputtered; Troy said that he couldn't send them to the principal's office — not yet. I liked the "not yet"; it was like Troy knew it was inevitable, but still — not yet. Mr. Truelove, unblinking, said, "Yeah, I can." And off they went, shaking their heads at this unexpected display of zero tolerance from the new guy. When the door closed behind them, Truelove turned to the rest of us. "Being here is optional. Paying attention is not."

Dell whispered to me, "He doesn't even look the least bit discomfited," which is the kind of thing she comes up with at times like this, and I laughed out loud, causing TL (as I now thought of him) to turn his piercing green eyes in my direction. Funny how a person becomes more attractive when they're being masterful.

"Something you would like to share with the class, Ms. ... er ... Miner-Cooper?" he asked, glancing quickly at the seating chart.

Too soon to tell who this guy was, but not too soon to see that he was pretty quick when it came to dispatching people to the principal's office. I didn't even know where the principal's office was. I made a quick judgment call. "Well, my friend was saying," I began, but Dell coughed discreetly. "I mean, I was just saying ... to myself" — I tossed an equally discreet glare at Dell — "that you didn't look in the least discomfited by that, um, little thing ..."

"Exchange," Dell stage-whispered, while giving

me a dirty look for saying anything. It doesn't matter how judgmental she is being — she can't resist a word. (A word in need, she says, is a word indeed.)

"Exchange," I said, nodding. "And I would have to agree." He was looking curious now. "With myself." Now he looked amused. "So, to sum up ... nicely done."

Some of the kids laughed, in an appreciative way, I thought. Most seemed uninterested.

"Thank you for the affirmation," he smiled. "You might want to keep an eye on that whole talking-to-yourself thing." He twirled his finger near his ear — the universal sign for crazy. But he winked at the same time and it wasn't creepy or smarmy.

"I'll do that." (I was impressed by the gesture. My mom would never do that. She doesn't use "crazy" or "nuts" or "wacko" to describe her clients. She prefers "work in progress.")

"You have shown the insight, not to mention vocabulary, that I will expect from the students of this class," he continued. Then he went on to say that during this year it would be reasonable for us to expect to understand and eliminate some of the inconsistencies, insecurities, conflicts and unacceptable impulses that are part of life. This, he assured us, would assist in making our relations with others smoother and more rewarding and should enable us to better understand the puzzling responses we often observed in our families, friends and even casual acquaintances.

As I wrote all this down, word for word, I thought you really couldn't get better value than that out of a class. Who needed to spell when you could eliminate inconsistencies, insecurities, conflicts and unacceptable impulses? Who needed to add and subtract when we could have smoother and more rewarding relations with others? And how was Earth Science going to help us to better understand the puzzling responses we observed in our families, friends and even casual acquaintances?

I beamed at Dell, convinced that she would be sharing in the light of this epiphanous news, at the same time making a mental note to share the word "epiphanous" with her later and maybe check to see if it was a real word. But she was not beaming. She was scribbling on a tiny scrap of paper that she handed to me while TL gazed deeply somewhere else.

I glanced down at the short message: *So much for keeping a low profile.* On the bottom she'd drawn a version of a smiley face, only it was not smiley; it was actually quite demonic-looking. I'd already forgotten the new-school-entry policy we'd agreed on this morning. I gave her a mea culpa shrug and stuffed the message inside my pencil case. She'd get over it once the import of Mr. Truelove's words hit her. We were about to embark on an amazing journey that would enhance our understanding of self and others. And, by the end of the year, could we expect to understand everything that we, and others, did and said?

In the words of Mr. Truelove, "By and large, yes!"

• • •

Dell and I found a table in the farthest corner of the crowded cafeteria. When I saw Sam enter the room, I stood up and waved for him to come over.

"Again, the concept of low profile seems to be one that you have absolutely no grasp on." She slurped her chocolate milk.

"He can't find us if he can't find us, now can he?" I asked. She didn't reply. I looked around the table of people who looked more or less as out of place as we did. "Was anyone here discomfited by my waving motion?"

Nobody said a thing. Dell had to smile. Chocolate milk wasn't exactly coming out of her nose, but it was a genuine smile. "That comment was for your ears only and you know it. I can't believe you got credit for it. Good vocabulary, my big butt."

"I thought TL handled the whole thing really well."

"TL?"

"Sure. Doesn't he look like he deserves an abbreviation?"

"No. Not hardly. Do you have a thing for him?"

"No." As far as Dell was concerned, there were two types of males in the world: guys you had a thing for and guys you didn't. "But I feel strongly about this."

She thought a moment. "Okay. But LT, okay? It's less conspicuous."

"Less discomfiting?"

"You're wearing out the new word."

"Fine. LT."

"Hey, Sam," she said.

Sam had found his way to us with his lunch tray intact. He had a shirt on that screamed first day of school. It was crumpled in exactly the same way it must have been pre-crumpled by the kind marketing people at American Eagle. No matter. He was looking very cute. One day I would tell our kids about how cute their dad looked on the day our love affair became public. "Hi, Sam. How are you?" I could feel Dell's hot stare on my face.

Sam returned the smile and put his tray beside mine. He climbed onto the bench beside me. So this was what it felt like to have a boyfriend: somebody automatically sat in the seat next to you without even asking. Maybe I was letting him take me for granted? Maybe this was presumptuous? No, it was too soon for second thoughts. We hadn't even had our first date yet. Only one dance — interrupted by his barfing brother.

"I am fine," Sam said. "How are you?"

"Good Lord," Dell said. "It's happened. Why is the best friend the last to know?"

"You were out of town until last night," I said. "And nothing's happened," I added, overwhelmed with guilt that I hadn't at least e-mailed to tell her that Sam and I were an about-to-happen situation, in keeping with our "withhold nothing" friendship policy.

"*She said*, apparently unaware that he was sitting right beside her," said Sam.

"I'm so not unaware of that," I said in a very sexy kind of way. For me, that is. This whole boyfriend thing is virgin territory for me, if you know what I mean.

"Good Lord," Dell said again. "When did this happen?"

"Nothing happened," I insisted again, trying to balance the whole sexy if-you-know-what-I-mean thing with Sam along with the you're-my-best-friend-I-tell-you-everything with Dell. "That's it. I suck at this. I give up."

Sam smiled. I have seen that smile in so many places in my life: across a playpen, a stroller, a sandbox — in a drama class when he was Aladdin and I was somebody in a veil. I've seen that smile encased in a set of plastic double blocks so he couldn't talk properly, and then in braces when I had to turn away for fear of losing my lunch after looking at the remains of his. I've seen that smile my whole life. It just never, ever did to me before what it was doing to me now.

"So we're breaking up?" Sam said. "Before our first date?"

"I could give you another chance." I said, clearly getting better at this whole seductive-sexy thing. Must be the two inches I grew during summer. Not to mention my bust line, which had gone from a hint to a definite suggestion.

"I have to go," Dell said suddenly.
"Don't," I said.
"Yeah," Sam said.
"See you later," I called to her retreating back.

Chapter Two

By and large, I would say that it's bad form to rub your best friend's face in your new relationship when her relationship has just dissolved or, as my dad would say, been flushed down the crapper.

Ever since Marshall (her ex) and Über-Angela, Dell's been turned off men. In the last two weeks, Dell broke up with Marshall for his cadlike behavior and reconciled with me — after being mad because I told her about said behavior. And now she has to digest the news that I have an almost-boyfriend: Sam. That's a lot to take. Bottom line: I needed to stop by Dell's house to see how she was doing.

• • •

After four rings, she opened the door. There was no welcoming aroma of baking cookies, which meant that her father had finally found a plot to his new book.

"So, literature's gain is our loss ... cookie-wise, I mean," I said cleverly. Dell just looked at me. Her eyes told me nothing; her body language was silent. She was learning to combat my secret powers.

"How could you not tell me about you and Sam? How?" She spun on her heels.

I followed her inside. "I haven't seen a move like that since you did the ballerina thing."

I only bring up the ballerina thing when I need to remind her that she owes me one. (There was a tutu, a boy with a tuba, a can of tuna. Actually, there was no tuna. But there was Dell in a tutu on a stage and a boy in the orchestra pit and there was disaster and I never speak of it unless I have to remind her of lifelong friendship.)

She spun again. "There will be no talk of the ballet." She raised her chin in a haughty manner.

"I'm just reminding you that — "

"I know, I know. I danced off the stage into the orchestra pit where Tuba-boy broke my fall and you never, ever told another living soul because you're such a friggin' saint."

I smiled. "I'm sorry I didn't tell you about me and Sam. But you were out of town and really there isn't any me and Sam yet. But I think there might be. Do you think there should be?"

"Yes."

I gave a sigh of relief. "Really?"

"Of course."

I told her about the dance at the wedding and the twinkly lights and the ganache and the barfing. She said she thought it said a lot about Sam that he wasn't able to kiss me after his little brother had been physically ill and I agreed. Then she said that she could practically feel the heat between us at the cafeteria today and I thought *I* might get physically ill.

"Are you okay?" she asked.

"I think so."

"Do you need something? Smelling salts?"

"Because you have smelling salts under your bed," I said, pulling a pillow up against my stomach, which was twirling like a flushed toilet.

"No, but I have chocolate."

"Of course you do."

While we surveyed the selection of mini-bars in her chocolate minibar, she casually mentioned that she might give Marshall another chance. I was upside down at the time, so the blood kind of rushed to my head and I collapsed on the other side of the bed in a heap. She peered over with a look of concern on her face. But there was also a definite air of satisfaction that I couldn't remember seeing before.

"I say, I say, what?" A cartoon voice was the best I could come up with.

"Everybody deserves a second chance, don't you think?"

"No, I don't."

"Yes, you do."

"I really don't."

"Have an Oh Henry!" She handed me her favorite mini-bar. "I think Marshall and I are back together again, definitely."

I tore the wrapper off and popped the whole bar in my mouth because (a) I was hungry and (b) then I couldn't speak and, as I was barely coming off a mea culpa situation, not speaking was probably good. "Why?" I finally said.

"You're judging me."

"I'm chewing."

"Chewing and judging."

"Remember that letter you wrote me about him? Misogynistic, you said. Roiling rot was also mentioned."

"That was a good letter."

"Roiling rot!"

"I've forgiven him."

I shook my head to try to get this piece of information to make sense. It didn't work. "Why?"

"He deserves another chance. Who was willing to give the evil stepsister another chance?"

Crap, I thought. "I was, am," I said. "But that's different. I have to give her another chance or live with ..." I groped around for the proper word. Proper words were important to Dell.

"Enmity? Rancor? Hostility?"

I held up my hand to stop her. "Thanks, Alex. I'll take 'enmity' for five hundred. Seriously, I have to live with her. I *need* to try to make it work. But you? Why do you *need* to give Marshall another chance? How did this happen?"

She slowly unveiled a Crispy Crunch and nibbled around the edges. "He said he was sorry."

Sarcasm welled up in my brain like an aneurysm. "Mhmm?"

"He said that Angela lunged at him."

"Hmm?"

"And that he just lost his mind for a second because she was looking really hot."

"Phhht." I couldn't help this. Air escaped from my mouth through no act of will of my own.

"I know. But then he kind of grabbed me by my shoulder, like this." Dell demonstrated, turning me toward her with a sudden move. "Only less jerky, and I wasn't staring up at him with scary eyes."

"I'm not looking at you with scary eyes. I am looking at you with objective social-scientist eyes."

She snorted. "I can't explain love, Jes. Who can explain love?"

"Oh. Oh." I raised my arm. "I can. Do you remember at the PNE last year, when we went on the Ferris wheel?"

She nodded.

"How did it make you feel?"

"I puked."

"Exactly. So then we went on the Scrambler and the Octopus and the stupid Teacup ride. And you were fine, right?"

"Yes."

"But then we walked past the Ferris wheel and you wanted to go again."

"I get the point, but it's so not the point."

"It so is so the point. You wanted to go on it again and we did and what happened?"

"I puked."

I waved my arms around my head wildly. "I rest my case."

"You have no case."

"How can you say that? You puked on my new runners."

"Well, the point is I wanted to go again *despite* the fact that it made me puke. It was *still* worth it."

"Hmm."

Dell looked proud.

"So love makes you puke?" I asked.

She smiled. "I think maybe it does."

Chapter Three

Jumping off the rope at Mara last summer was my first time. Ever. Most kids try it when they're seven or eight years old. They swing out from the cliff over the water and let go. Sam was five, but he's a show-off so he doesn't count. Dell was seven. (Also a show-off.) I like to think of myself as not a show-off, but that's not why I didn't do it until last summer at the embarrassing age of fifteen. I didn't do it until then because I was afraid of breaking my neck. Fear of falling, fear of pain. Classic.

• • •

Dell's unappealing words of love wisdom clanged around in my head as I drew closer to my house. From a block away, I could see brightly colored Cal — festooned in spandex and Lycra and other technologically advanced fabrics created to keep the sweat he worked so hard to create from reaching his skin — climbing the stairs. He hoisted his bike like a briefcase. (Extremely light, more space-age materials.) Cal has painstakingly explained all the wind-resistant benefits of his outfit, but he still looks like a guy in tights. Add a pair of pointy-toed shoes and a tutu and ... no, not kind. A bow and arrow. He could be a modern-day Robin Hood, or a merry man, at least. Cal was quite merry, I reminded myself. These were the things a newly minted optimist needed to reinforce.

In the front entrance, I stepped around the unpacked boxes that had been arriving gradually throughout the last couple of months. Cal had his apartment for a while yet and he'd been bringing stuff over one box at a time. My mom wondered about this in a gentle, lighthearted way, or at least what she considers gentle and lighthearted but is actually a smiley version of *Why don't you just move in already?*

Then there were Angela's boxes that arrived via Greyhound bus from California. (They got unpacked, flattened, sorted into recycling bins within, I think, five minutes.) Her mother had no trouble agreeing to Angela living here, but took her time in sending the stuff. Angela said it was typical. Apart from telling me that her mother never showed up to watch her soccer games, Angela doesn't really talk much about her, which is a bit of a mystery, I guess. Not a mystery I'm particularly intrigued with, but maybe I should be? Maybe that's a part of being extended, blended.

We may be an officially blended family, but we were really still at the ice-crunching stage. If our blender is any indication, we could eventually expect to stir, chop, mix, liquefy and puree. Then there's the pulse option. The objective being that at the end of it all we would be one big smoothie. Sounds messy to me.

When I was a kid, I would have thought I'd gone to fort heaven with all these boxes. A person could construct an entire village. As I navigated around a particularly large box, I peeked inside and saw a large-screen TV. I felt encouraged. Maybe there was a new stereo system here as well. Maybe it was time to move up to "mix" on the old blender. I could practically feel Mr. Truelove's approval at what was surely a mature and insightful step in the direction of mental health.

"Jes, is that you?" My mother appeared in the doorway of the kitchen and then disappeared as quickly. Was she wearing an apron? I must be seeing things. It would be an odd kind of mirage. She's not a big fan of cooking — hates it, actually. If you want to hear her go on about how a pair of ovaries has nothing to do with an ability to cook, suggest that cooking is woman's work. (Sometimes I say it just for fun.) Plus you'll get to see her turn a number of shades of red blotch. "Tell me about your day," she called.

The kitchen was also full of boxes, but a quick glance inside made me think that they were on their way out. While my mother is not a good cook, she does enjoy creating the appearance of good cooking. Cal's collection of old Tupperware and plastic sour cream containers (who saves sour cream containers?)

and mismatched, chipped dishes were not going to support the illusion.

She was indeed wearing an apron, but this was nothing next to the fact that she was wrestling with a piece of meat the size of her head. "Roast beef," she said triumphantly.

I slid onto one of the bar stools at the counter.

"And Yorkshire pudding and mashed potatoes with gravy and carrots with ginger and chocolate cake for dessert."

"That sounds great," I said. "But what have you done with my mother? She's about so tall, blue eyes. Usually wears a business suit?" I glanced around the kitchen. "Never goes anywhere without cream of mushroom soup?"

She shook her head. "That's the old Elli. The new Elli is through with shortcuts."

"The new Elli?"

"That's right. The one who is learning to embrace the minutiae of everyday life."

"Embrace the huh-what?"

"Smell the roses, listen to the birds, watch the grass grow." She smiled in a manner that indicated she thought she was making sense.

"Okay," I said. "What about watching boiling pots?"

"Sure. Why not! Although they do say a watched pot never —"

"Er, I meant the pot behind you." Something was belching steam and water all over the stove.

"Oh, potatoes!" She grabbed a pot holder. She pulled the pot off the element, fiddled with the dial and propped the lid on its side. "And sometimes an unwatched pot spills over everything."

I smiled, reassured that the new Elli could turn everything into a life lesson. A lot like the old Elli. I grabbed an apple from the bowl.

"Dinner is in half an hour — don't ruin your appetite," she said, still looking at the pot as if defying it to boil over again. Also like the old Elli. "And tell Angela, will you? She's in her room."

"Yeah, yeah." Her room? My room, she meant. I'd given it to Angela in a wildly generous moment when I found out that she was moving in with us. I moved across the hall into my little sister's room. Every time I walked in, I expected to see Alberta popping up from her crib or scaling down the side of it the way she had just learned to do. I told myself it was just a room, a place to sleep and hold my clothes, but I couldn't shake the old feeling that I was in the wrong place.

Upstairs, I threw my backpack inside where it was swallowed whole by the messiness. That was mine, at least. "A messy room shows a messy mind," my mom always said. Yep.

I knocked on Angela's door. Her music was weird: wooden flutes, sitars and forest noises. Little bit spooky. I knocked louder.

"Come in."

The door opened easily because Angela, unlike

myself, kept a very orderly room. (And an orderly mind?) She dusted, vacuumed and straightened every Saturday at ten o'clock in the morning. She stopped at the door, though, and often left the vacuum out for me, "just in case."

"Hey," I said. She was sitting in the middle of her immaculate floor in a position that didn't look humanly possible. One leg was wrapped around her neck so that her foot was actually facing me. I twisted my head around to see if it would make more sense. It didn't. "What are you doing?"

"Creating a vessel into which light can flow."

"Oh."

"The stars do it all the time."

"Like Orion or the Big Dipper?"

"Funny. Actually, it's a way to get in touch with the Eternal Now."

"That sounds like a really long time."

"Can I help you?" She smiled politely from within her pretzeled self. When she wasn't stealing boyfriends or smuggling shoplifted necklaces into my backpack (and then denying that she did it), she was generally polite. That was too negative. I needed to remember the new optimistic me.

"Dinner is in half an hour ... from now. Not the Eternal Now, though, just regular now. My mom wanted me to tell you."

"Thanks." She lifted the other leg and wrapped it, too, around her neck. I couldn't help staring. It was mesmerizing.

"Doesn't that hurt?" I said.

"No." She shrugged and her legs bounced along with her shoulders. Okay, now it was starting to freak me out. "I can show you how to do this."

"Thanks, maybe later." She smiled like she might be taking me seriously. "You just, uh, let your light flow," I said.

"You should really try this," she called after me. "It's great for the abs."

Maybe my less-than-rock-hard abs had been insulted, but I wasn't quite sure. Go new me.

• • •

The gravy was lumpy, the potatoes were runny, the meat was tough. As I sawed away, I tried to think of something to say because my mom had that look on her face. You know the one: the Christmas-morning look, the birthday-present look, the report-card-day look. The universal hopeful-mother look.

"Great veggies, Elli," said Angela, finding the one possible true compliment. "Absolutely perfect."

Cal murmured agreeably as he sawed.

"Can I pass you the meat, Angela?" Mom said.

Angela smiled pleasantly. "I'm sorry, I should have told you. I've gone macrobiotic."

I stabbed a large piece of meat and jammed it into my mouth. I was chewing when my mom glanced my way, as I knew she would. I shrugged and smiled.

"Macrobiotic?" she said.

"It's a dietary wellness system based on whole foods."

My mother smiled through narrowed eyes.

"It acknowledges the inter-relationship among body, mind and spirit," Angela continued.

And here my mom thought that it would be enough to create a well-balanced meal, when she should have been balancing body, mind and spirit. I was glad that I was still chewing. I waited to hear what my mother would say. Angela had no idea how rare it was for my mother to put together a meal like this.

"That's great, Angela. Maybe we should all try that."

I swallowed too soon and had to grab my glass of water so that the lump of partially masticated meat didn't choke me to death. My mom patted me on the back. She asked if I was okay and gave me the sterling advice to "chew before you swallow." Before I knew it, I seem to have said something about how I wouldn't have to chew a hundred times if I didn't have to eat leather. Something like that. I don't really remember because then my mother's face turned lime green and she ran out of the room.

How did this happen? How? I had such a good attitude and everything. I got up to follow her.

"It's okay, Jes. I'll go," Cal said, and then he was gone as well.

Angela looked at me sympathetically. She reminded me of the Good Witch in *The Wizard of Oz* (who, by the way, if she was such a good witch, should have told Dorothy right away that all she needed to do was smack her feet together. She'd have been back in

Kansas in time for supper. Probably not overcooked, either.) "It's an adjustment," she said, delicately chewing her carrot.

We finished our meal in silence. I was thinking, How did things go so terribly wrong? Angela was probably thinking, Gee, I'm smart. And beautiful. And thin. And well-behaved. And flexible.

• • •

To continue the mea culpa trend of the day, I cleaned up the kitchen when Cal and my mother did not return to the dinner table. Angela passed on dessert after reminding me that refined white sugar was only one of the many ways that yin and yang become unbalanced.

I was wiping the last bit of gravy off the counter when Cal walked back into the room. He pushed his hand through his hair as though he had some. (He'd voluntarily shorn, it either as a further commitment to wind resistance or maybe to look like Lance Armstrong.) "Can you come into the living room, Jes? Your mother and I have something we want to say."

I followed him. Angela was sitting beside my mom. I noticed that she was still a little green. (My mother, not Angela, who was rosy and brimming with good health.)

"I'm sorry," I said immediately, getting it out of the way. I couldn't stand the thought of a family meeting. "I really have some homework that I should get to." I was about to launch into the whole good and productive life beginning with good and productive homework speech when my mother's face stopped me cold. She actually looked like she was sick and my heart stopped for a second. "Are you okay?" I asked.

"Jes, Angela. Your dad and I — I mean, Cal and I ..." She swiveled her head between the two of us; I knew she was trying to say whatever she was trying to say the right way, offending no one. She stopped, expelled any leftover breath. "Let me start again. We didn't mean for this to happen ... so soon. Of course, there's no way of knowing these things. But I'm almost forty years old, right, Jes?"

I was eager to help, if only to get this over with and back upstairs again, door closed. I had never wanted to finish my homework more in my life. "Yes," I agreed. "Almost forty."

"That's right. And you're fifteen. And Angela is sixteen. And we know — Cal and I — I mean, your dad and I."

"Yeah, Mom. Got that. The two of you. Tick tock."

"Just let her finish, Jes," Cal said in a tone that I had never heard from him before. Tense, controlled and just this side of shrill. The psychologist version of pissed off.

I was regular pissed off. Mom appeared dismayed. Angela looked as though the Buddha himself was shining light into the vessel of herself. (Would the Buddha look smug, though? I don't think so.)

Mom hurried ahead. "It's just that we realize the two of you are at a very delicate point in your development. And this could be unsettling, but we hope it won't be. We hope that you'll see it the way we do. A gift, really."

I looked at Angela, wondering if her new balanced yin and yang understood what was going on, but she was expressionless.

"We're pregnant," Cal said.

Chapter Four

"You said that?" Dell said with a gasp.

I didn't think the gasp was necessary and told her so. "I don't remember if I said that exactly ... it was all a blur. This whole thing has been very upsetting."

"Well, sure, but you told them to check with you the next time they have any birth-control questions? And then you listed the options?"

"I don't remember ... it's growing very dim in here. Like I could lose consciousness any minute." I leaned back on her bed. It didn't seem like it had only been a few hours since I was here last. Back then, my biggest problem was making sure Dell was okay and wondering about my still-to-come first date with Sam. Ah, life was so simple then ... three hours ago.

Dell paced back and forth, chewing the inside of her cheek — gross — which she does when she is trying to figure something out. "This is tricky, my friend. Very tricky. We need to go back to the beginning. Cal said, 'We're pregnant.' Then what happened?"

"I told you. I said, 'We?' And he blushed all the way up the back of his neck ..."

"Oh, I hate that."

"Why do you hate that?"

"Vulnerable parents are the worst. It makes you feel sorry for them, often when you need to hate them the most. It's not fair."

"That's right! It's not fair! I felt like such a cow, but I couldn't stop myself. My mom was looking at me with those stupid Dr. Dolittle Seal Eyes and ..."

"Whoa, I don't know that one. Dr. Dolittle Seal Eyes?"

"Yes, you do. Remember when Dr. Dolittle is going to return Sophie the seal to the ocean because it's her true home and her seal lover is waiting for her, but then they have this moment where he starts singing to her: 'When I look into your eyes I see the world ...' or something like that? Oh, Dell, stop it." She was starting to brim up with tears. "It's not the point."

"It was a very good scene. I remember it now."

I nodded. "Do you need a moment? A tissue? Some time to get over Dr. Dolittle and his seal friend and a scene that was actually a little too romantic for a man and a marine mammal — if you know what I mean?"

"I'm fine," she said. "Continue."

"So my mom looks at me and I know she wants me to do something or say something else, something better, and I thought, This isn't my job. It's not my job to make this better for you."

"And that's when you said that if they had any questions about birth control they should have come to you. Condoms, diaphragm, the pill, etc."

I nodded, cringing now that the moment had

passed. So many thoughts had crowded into my mind. Me — six years old. My mom and dad saying, "You're going to have a little baby something." They laughed when they said it and explained that they meant I was going to have a baby brother or sister, but by then I already thought that they meant a puppy. I don't know why. A puppy was a baby something.

It only took a second for me to get over my disappointment because they looked so happy and, I don't know, shiny. I couldn't understand how two people could look that way. It was too much; it overwhelmed me and I started to cry. But they thought I was crying because of the new baby and they said, both of them, that nobody would ever replace me. They would always love me. And the whole thing got very confusing because I wasn't crying because of a new baby or even a new puppy. I was crying because of how shiny and happy they looked.

All of that came rushing back when Cal said "we." I thought I'd already adjusted to the new we, but I guess this was the new and improved we. Then I got mad because now I had to adjust all over again. Thoughts like this don't come in order, though. They come in an avalanche. All you can do is try to jump out of the way and hope you're wearing the jacket with the homing device in the lining.

"I probably should have just said 'Congratulations,'" I said. "That would have been better."

"Probably."

• • •

When I returned to the house, a couple of hours and a lot of chocolate later, my mother was waiting for me in the living room. Some of the boxes had been removed and the large-screen TV was set up in the corner of the room. They'd been busy.

"Honey, can I talk to you?" she said.

"Could we do it in the morning?"

"We could. I'd rather do it now."

Sensible Mom. Sensible, in-control Mom. Sensible, in-control, knocked-up Mom. "Okay," I said. I sat down on the overstuffed chair and covered it with my outstretched body. Every part of me needed to rest.

"I need you to be okay with this," she said.

"Then I'm okay with this. I have homework to do."

She closed her eyes slowly and sat there with her eyes shut. "I really need you to be okay with this."

I saw the tears that squeezed out of the corners of her closed lids, but I couldn't deal with them. "Then I really am."

She didn't say anything, didn't open her eyes. I pulled myself up off of the chair and left the room.

• • •

I wasn't in bed more than two and a half minutes when a knock came at the door. I asked who it was, thinking I knew who it was, and then it wasn't who I thought it was. It was Angela. In the weeks we'd officially been an extended blended, she had never knocked on my door.

"Come in."

She stood at the door wearing rubber gloves, which I thought was strange. But then, if she thought it was strange that I was under my covers with all my clothes on, she didn't say. "I just wanted you to know that I cleaned the bathroom."

"Oh. Thanks."

"It was incredibly dirty."

"Yes. I bet it was."

She didn't come in the room, or take off her gloves. I didn't invite her in, or explain why I was in the bed with all my clothes on. It was an awkward moment.

"So, uh, that was some kind of news," I ventured.

"Yeah, a sib," she said, and then she shrugged. "But the bathroom's clean. I just wanted to let you know."

"Thanks," I said.

She left in a blur of beauty and perfection, even in the rubber gloves. I climbed out of bed and avoided looking at myself in my mirror. Then, I thought that maybe I didn't really need to look at myself anymore. I grabbed an extra blanket and draped it over the mirror above my chest of drawers. The room immediately felt cozier and more personal, like a cave. Really, in a rapidly growing household, it was probably important to grab any inch of space there was. I didn't want to share anymore, not even with a reflection of me.

Chapter Five

Once upon a time, the continents fit together, but, over time, they have drifted apart. That's how the story goes. Every bit of dirt and grass and hill and bump was once compressed into a single protocontinent called Panagaea — all lands. Plate tectonics. Scraping patterns and mid-oceanic ridges and geomagnetic anomalies. And an ever-present teaching tool — a guiding light — in our spreading, cracking household. The details confuse me, but I like the ideas (and I'm very proud of my metaphor — Dell would be pleased), especially the one about convection currents that lie beneath the plates. These currents move the crustal plates in different directions. The source of the heat that drives the convection is radioactivity deep in the Earth's mantle.

Think about it: as the ocean floor is spread apart, cracks allow molten magma to surface and form the newest ocean floor. And as the old ocean floor moves away from the mid-oceanic ridge, it will eventually slip beneath a continental plate. Finally, the plates will get driven down and return to a heated state.

I wasn't sure who was who in our domestic scenario

of geological wonderment, only that our crust was being spread apart. Again. Sure to return to a heated state. Readily, under stress.

• • •

The next couple of days went by without any major geological incident. In the morning, two of us trundled off to school, one of us glazed himself in wind-resistant synthetic material and whistled off to work and the other of us stayed home to puke. None of us talked about the molten news that was convecting us into something new.

My mom, when not being lime green, was doing her rubber ball thing: bouncing back. Now that the news was out, she acted as though this was the happy plan all along. She is big on plans, big on happy, big on acting.

Now that I'd had time to think about it — the new molten baby — I was pretty sure I hated the idea. But I didn't hate it in a negative way because that would be out of keeping with my new, optimistic, hope-seeking self. I simply hated the idea in a completely objective, scientific way — no judgment, no hard feelings, no resentment, no thoughts of revenge. It was a pure kind of hatred that I didn't quite understand, but that was okay because this wasn't about logic. It was about gut. My gut was telling me that nothing good would come of it.

• • •

I buzzed Dad a good long time before static responded on his building's ancient intercom system.

"Sorry ... fuzzzz ... buying groceries ... fuzzzy. Come in ... fuzzzzzzz."

I lunged for the door when I heard the buzz, but I missed that delicate moment between the buzz and the click because the length of time allotted to opening the door was infinitesimal. A cheetah would have a problem reaching the door in time, although I thought I'd mastered it. Clearly, I was slipping. I was about to call Dad to try again when a man came up and unlocked the door with his key. I was preparing to give him my most winning smile to reassure him that I was not a young offender so that he would let me in, rather than continue this stupid farce of buzz and run, when I realized that the man was Mr. Truelove. My smile, as they say, froze on my face and I said, brilliantly, "You? You live here?"

"I was tired of living in the gym with the rest of the teachers." He held the door open for me. "Did you want to come in?"

"Oh, no," I said automatically.

He looked puzzled. "Okay, then."

I grabbed the door before it closed and followed him in. "But I could, I guess. I mean, I will. Sure. Thanks."

"No problem." He pressed the button at the elevator and gave me a sideways glance. "But I have to say you seemed a little more comfortable with the English language the other day."

I smiled apologetically and wondered how obvious it would look if I took the stairs to avoid him. But I was already standing in front of the elevator. It would look completely obvious. While I was deciding, the doors opened and he motioned for me to go ahead, with the same courtly gesture he had used to send Troy and Flynn to the principal's office. This put things into perspective nicely: *me teacher, you lowly pupil.* I entered the cramped cubicle.

It was permeated with the smell of the hallways and presented the usual conundrum: who was cooking what tonight? (I once made the mistake of assuming that Mr. Singh was preparing curry and Ms. Smith was cooking pork chops and somehow this came up during a lurching elevator ride. Both Mr. Singh and Ms. Smith chided me on my assumptions. Stereotyping, they said, almost in sync. By the time we reached our common floor, I was promising them that I would never ever assume a spice/culture connection again.)

"Smells like Thai tonight," he smiled. "Green curry, I think."

"Good nose," I said, because I had to say somthing. But did I have to comment on a personal body part? What was wrong with me? Maybe next I'd blurt out that he had a nice ass. You never know what you're going to say in times of stress. I quickly tried to think of something non-body-part related. A paperback peeked out of his jacket pocket. *Hamlet.* Aha.

This was the slowest elevator in the world and he had pressed eleven. I was going to the tenth floor.

This meant lots of time to get to know each other, lots of time for him to ask me questions if I didn't strike first. "You're reading that? We read it last year. I thought it was boring, at first, but then I kind of liked it." Third floor.

"Ophelia was a bit of a wimp," I raced on, "and I really didn't like that whole double standard where she's supposed to be the good girl but old Laertes can just fool around with whoever he wants. What's that about?" Fifth floor. Mr. Truelove was looking at me like I'd lost my mind. "Talk about your dysfunctional family, right? Hey, Hamlet, talk to yourself much? Plus you got a brother killing his own brother then marrying the wife — who he's been fooling around with, thank you very much — and then Dad's ghost tells his own kid that he has to kill his uncle out of revenge. *Thanks, Dad. Just the way I wanted to spend the rest of my life.* Sheesh. What's with Shakespeare? And does *everybody* have to die? I was really rooting for Hamlet, but noooo. Everybody dies." Ninth floor.

"Hamlet dies?" said Mr. Truelove.

I was horrified. "Oh, God, I'm sorry. You're not there yet? You didn't know?"

He smiled then in a way that made him almost handsome and it totally threw me off. Not that I wasn't already off. "I'm kidding," he said.

"Oh, good one," I said. Tenth floor. The doors parted to reveal sweet freedom. "My floor," I said.

"Are you up to your destiny?"

"Huh?" I stared at him through the narrowing space of the closing doors.

And then the doors shut, just like the curtains in a theater. Dell would love that.

• • •

I knocked on the door and walked into the apartment at the same time. "Honey, I'm home," I yelled. It was our new routine. We used to have a relationship; now we have a routine.

When you are a child of divorce — a product of the great divide — you learn to be flexible and creative. You learn that it's not the expected, but the unexpected, that is the spice of life. I have tried to add a pinch of sitcom to my *Father/Daughter: The Later Years*. If I could pull together a theme song that would play when I entered the room, I would do it. It would say, "This is the new us, the new life," but in a jaunty, merry fashion — as seen on TV.

I never knew that our old life didn't exist the way I thought it did until my parents explained they had decided to divorce. Divorce: to sever one thing from another. Or, as I like to think of it: instant plate tectonics. You think you're one continent? Wrongo. Now you're two. There was ice cream and talk of dissolving and chocolate sauce and separate paths.

What I remember, after all the talking, after the decrees (that's what you get when you divorce, a decree, probably signed by Julius Caesar), is that I felt like the knot in the middle of a tug-of-war rope. Never quite knew which side of the line I was going to be pulled across. But I have to give them credit — they both kept tugging to make sure the knot (me, in case you forgot) was on their side. Eventually, I found it kind of touching and meaningful. And I think I assumed they would keep tugging. But now there was a new little knot in the picture. And three people tugging. It was a whole new game.

"What's for supper?" I said, sniffing the air.

"Dolmades, for one thing."

"Sounds like a mountain range," I said.

"Stuffed grape leaves."

"How do you stuff a leaf?"

"Hmm. Excellent question. Because, the thing is, you actually roll the leaf around the rice mixture. There is no stuffing involved."

"You've been duped."

He smiled and gave me a kiss on the forehead. "It looks that way."

"Smells good, though. What's with the beige goop?"

"Hummus. Chick peas. It's a little runny. But the tzatziki ..."

"Gesundheit."

"Thank you. The tzatziki is wonderful. Then there's moussaka. And for dessert — baklava!" Somehow he felt that this pronouncement required jazz hands. Jazz hands and a goofy look on his face.

"And that is?"

"Honey and wafers and nuts and stuff."

"Mom's pregnant — did you know?" I meant to say that the dinner sounded fabulous and amazing. Maybe it was the baklava that led me to my proclamation. Honey: a sticky substance that held onto something. Wafers: like layers of the earth crust. Nuts and stuff: we were all nuts. It all added up to my blurtation: *did you know?* But I knew. I knew he didn't know. I could just tell by the way he was so happy when I came into the apartment that he didn't know. And then I felt the hate all over again for why it had to be this way. Why, Shakespeare, why? You're the big tragedy-genius. Why does it work this way?

My dad said nothing at first. He just took the plate away and stepped the four steps necessary to enter the kitchenette. (That's what it's called in an apartment. It's a demeaning term.) "Holy Moses in the Desert, I think the dolmades are burning."

Personally, I wasn't sure if this was an expression that was going to catch on worldwide, but it did reek of newness. I watched him pull a tray of blackened matter out of the oven. "So you didn't know?"

"Dolmade?" he said, shoving the tray in my direction.

I took a steaming leaf off the tray, remembering that I'd seen them in the coolers at the Greek/Mediterranean/Israeli section in the deli at the grocery store. "Are they supposed to be cooked?" I asked.

"Well, I assumed."

"Okay." I took a bite of the desiccated thumb-shaped morsel. The rice was crisp and burned. "Yum."

"I know how you like to try new foods." He smiled sheepishly.

There it was: the vulnerable-parent look. He was trying to make me happy with a Greek feast. I gulped and swallowed. Just stick a poisoned sword into my gut; it would be quicker. "But did you know?"

He took a grape-leaf thing and popped it into his mouth. I recognized the exit strategy immediately. "Hmm hmmm," he said. But his eyes said something else. I hadn't seen those eyes in a long time and I cursed myself for not thinking quicker, sooner. If I had really thought about it, I never would have asked. I would have kept it to myself the way Hamlet, Sr., should have kept his big fat ghost trap shut. *Get over it, already. You're dead. You're a ghost.* My dad's eyes looked sorrowful and they brimmed with regret. Dr. Dolittle Seal Eyes. "No, I didn't."

The whole scenario was over in a second — a blink. By the time he had Greek salad on the table his eyes were normal again, but time is funny that way. It stops during the sad parts — even without the cue of a theme song or soliloquy.

I babbled about school. I told him about Mr. Truelove and the amazing elevator coincidence. I described the meeting down to the last humiliating detail. (Personal humiliation is well worth it if it gets rid of parental humiliation.) "You mean George?" Dad said.

"George?"

"Sounds like him. He moved in last month. He always has a book with him. That's how we started talking. Otherwise I'm not that sociable. It's a long elevator ride, have you noticed?"

"George?"

"Tall guy? Lanky."

I laughed. "Lanky. He just doesn't seem like a George to me. That's too, I don't know, too George Washington: wooden teeth, cherry trees, honest man. It's too simple."

"He doesn't seem like a simple man to you?"

Oh, no. My dad was giving me his teacher look. If my mom had a mad scientist side to her where she wanted to know every detail that was bleeping along in my brain, my dad, the ex-teacher, wanted to explore my imagination. I had learned early on that, at times like these, it was better to do like dogs do: roll over and play dead.

"He doesn't seem like a George."

Dad didn't blink. In this respect he was nothing like my mother. "Maybe Truelove isn't his real name either. Have you considered that? Maybe it's an assumed name?"

I said I thought that was completely possible. "Maybe he's wanted by the FBI? Came up with Truelove because he was on the fly, on the lam, running from the law."

"For forgery?" Dad suggested. "So he changed his name. That would be ironic."

"He's a new man," I said. "Turned a new leaf."

"A grape leaf?"

"Maybe," I laughed.

My dad looked pleased. And then he brought out the moussaka. The eggplant was chewy and the béchamel sauce was like he'd sprayed it with a can of hair spray, but he'd tried. I had to give him that.

For the rest of the evening we thought up possible crimes that Mr. Truelove (or whoever) might have committed. Anything to avoid talking about the other thing. The molten thing. But it was still with us when I kissed him good-bye at the curb outside my house. He didn't drive right away; he never did. He wanted to make sure I got inside okay, I guess. But I wondered if he was also thinking, Hey! That's my house! Why aren't I going inside? Why, again, am I driving away?

Chapter Six

I was cross-legged on my bed trying to remember why I wanted to prove Corollary 3 of the Chord Perpendicular Bisector Theorem when the inevitable knock came at the door. I never had dinner at Dad's without the inevitable knock. (And now the inevitable knocker was knocked up, so that was kind of ironic in a way that I couldn't prove any more than the Chord Perpendicular Bisector Theorem.)

"Can I come in?" she asked.

"Enter," I said.

But my mom was already in and already asking, "Can we talk?"

I pointed to the math book in my lap.

"It'll only be a minute."

I shut the book with a nod and a sigh. A confession was on the horizon and I tried to prepare myself. I tried to imagine how the Pope might feel after a long day at St. Peter's when one more sad, sinful guy — one more sad, sinful story — shows up and all you want is a hot bath and a Fresca. (Although the Pope probably drinks Coke.)

"I know we sprung this news on you," she began, sitting at the edge of my bed. "That wasn't the plan. It just happened — honestly. I didn't even know if I was still fertile."

I could practically feel the Pope Points fall from my grasp as I physically cringed at the word "fertile." I managed to say nothing, but I noticed that she looked pretty, which is a weird thing to notice mid-cringe. There it was: she was glowing. Just like the cliché. "You look nice," I said.

She looked surprised at this. "Thanks. I feel really good ... when I'm not throwing up."

"That's a sign of a healthy baby," I offered, again without intent. To my discomfort, she welled up with tears. "I think I heard that."

She nodded and I could see she was composing herself. She glanced around the room, restraining herself from commenting on the chaos. I gave her a couple of Pope Points for that. "Why is there a blanket on your mirror?"

"Psychology assignment," I said quickly.

Her mouth tweaked upward and then downward and I knew she was torn between saying "say more" and getting on with her mission. I guess she decided on the latter because, for the next three hundred years, the air was filled with a speech, a monologue, a soliloquy that explained the incredible misunderstanding that had permeated our household.

Finally I said, "Huh?"

"Okay." She took a breath: in the nose, out the mouth. (I wondered if she'd swiped some of Angela's self-help tapes.) "I wanted to tell you first. Well, not first because I had to tell Cal first, obviously."

"Obviously."

"No, not obviously, I guess. Actually, he was there when I took the test and so, technically, we found out together." She suddenly looked at me and blushed.

Pieces pushed together. "Yeah, got that. You were together when you peed on the stick."

She turned from pink to almost crimson. "Well, not quite, but fine. And I wanted to tell you next, but then we thought that Angela also deserved to know and ..."

I really didn't want to see what color followed crimson and I remembered that the best defense is a good offense. (Something my coach told me during my bleak soccer year, when it turned out that I was not as interested in sending a ball through an arbitrary space between two poles as I wasn't.) "Why didn't you tell Dad you're pregnant?"

"Oh."

"Yeah, thought so."

"I was going to."

"Excellent news. I'll tell him that the next time I see him because I'm the messenger, right? Too bad, though. People tend to shoot the messenger, have you noticed? Even when they don't want to. Funny how they look at you like you're dirt. But you couldn't have known that." I smiled, and I knew it was an ugly smile, but I couldn't help myself.

"You sound really angry."

She was going into therapist mode so I lay flat on my bed and folded my arms across my chest. "Yes, Doctor, and when I was two years old I had some serious potty-training issues. I think that's where my anger might be coming from. Let's blame the potty, shall we?"

"Okay, okay. Can you sit up, please? Look at me."

Lying flat on my back, looking up at the ceiling that was still covered with the stars we'd put up there, I remembered what I said to my soccer coach when he asked me to try, just try, to put the ball between the two posts. After, I'd walked off the field, never to return. He told my father that he'd never seen such a stubborn little girl in all his life. I remember that Dad smiled at this. "Why should I?" I said, then and now.

"I was going to tell him, Jes. I forgot that it was his night to have you over for dinner and things were crazy at work. I wasn't feeling well and it slipped my mind. I was still getting over your reaction."

I sat up at this. "*I'm* why you didn't tell him? This is *my* fault?"

"No, of course not. It's nobody's fault."

This is one of my mother's famous lines. It was right up there with *chew before you swallow*. Nobody's fault. No fault involved. Like it just happens all by itself.

"Guess what, Mom? Deep inside the earth's crust is a fault line. A lot of fault lines, actually. Around here, it's called the San Andreas Fault. And when it's agitated, earthquakes happen. Fault lines are embedded in the very core of the earth."

"I don't know what you're talking about."

"Never mind."

"Can we start again?"

Another do-over. "Then can I get back to my math?"

"I'm sorry I didn't tell your father about the ... my pregnancy. It was an oversight."

"Fine. What else?"

She glanced over to the side of the room, fixing her unusually messy hair. She seemed perplexed. "*Why* is that mirror covered?"

"Tick tock."

"This isn't a good time for you. You should go back to studying. I'm sorry I disturbed you."

"Just say it, okay? Whatever you have to say."

She took a deep breath. Ran her fingers through that messy hair. I could feel the prickle at the back of my neck. Vulnerable-parent look squared to infinity coming up. "We're going to need more space when the ... the baby arrives."

"You want my room back." I looked at her, disbelieving. "You want my room back?"

She looked back for just a second, then straightened her shoulders and cleared her throat. "It's just that it's next to our room and it's the smaller of the two. Otherwise I'd ask Angela to move. I really hate to ask you to do this, Jes. I wish we could afford a bigger place, but we can't. I might have to take some time off. Well, of course I will, when he arrives, but the doctor thinks—"

"He?"

She stopped short. "Right, um, he. I was going to tell you."

I started to shake. I pressed my hands together so that she wouldn't notice. "He?"

"Oh, Jes. I had my ultrasound today. This afternoon." Then she had to stop because she was tearing up, and I hated her for that. But I hated myself, too, so we were even. "It's not certain, of course, it's too soon, but the technician thought so. And I know so, honey, I do."

I held up my hand like a crosswalk guard. "It's okay." It was suddenly so completely official. "I get it. Not a problem. I'll move. Actually, this is perfect."

"Really?"

"Yeah. Dad's got that extra bedroom. He said it's fine if I move in with him. It's the perfect solution."

She looked at me and I decided that I was sick to death of the Dr. Dolittle Seal Eye look. It was not going to work on me anymore.

"He said it was fine?"

I also decided that silence was probably the best

option, at least until I could confirm that my dad would actually say what I said he had said.

"Jes?"

"Mom, this theorem is not going to solve itself," I said finally, pointing to my math book.

She got up with a heavy sigh. "I realize that I'm doing this badly, Jes. My timing is ... bad." She started to tear up again. "And I shouldn't cry. That's unfair to you. Oh. Okay." She put her hand on her forehead. "My head is a little, um, full. It's too full. We'll talk later." And with that, she left the room.

As soon as the door clicked shut and her footsteps faded, I dove for the telephone and I dialed. Somebody speaking Chinese answered. I said I was sorry, hung up and tried again. This time my father answered. "Hello?"

"Hey, Dad. Were you sleeping?"

"Nope. Just looking up some stuff on the Internet. Did you know that dolmades are traditionally served cold?"

"You don't say."

"I do. Oh well, I never pretended to be Greek, did I?"

"No, Dad, you didn't." Suddenly this whole thing seemed Greek to me.

"What's up?"

"I was just wondering that if I ever needed a place to stay, I could totally stay with you, right?"

"Of course."

"So that would be fine?"

"It would be great."

"Okay. But it would be fine, right?"

"Of course."

"Of course what?"

"Of course, ma'am?"

"Is it too much to ask for you to say that it would be fine if I lived with you."

"It would be fine," he said. "What's going on?"

"Nothing. Just a math problem."

"Math?"

I proceeded to explain what little I knew about the Chord Perpendicular Bisector Theorem until he was good and confused, which managed to bisect the real reason for calling. We hung up with my traditional, "Love you."

"To the stars," he added.

I spent the rest of the evening with my book in my lap, looking up at sticky paper stars that wouldn't shine until the light was off.

Chapter Seven

Sam was on one side, Dell on the other, as we walked to school. I was explaining to them that our route might have to change slightly when I moved in with my dad. But other than that, nothing would change. Neither of them said much as I rambled on about how this would be the best solution ever. I talked about embracing change.

"Well, this is another fine mess you've gotten us into," Dell finally said.

"Huh?"

"Laurel and Hardy. My dad's been watching them nonstop. He's having 'theme' problems. Oh to have a normal father."

"Waaah." Sometimes Dell's so-called problems pissed me off. She had no idea about real problems.

Dell looked stricken. "Sorry. This is bigger. Sorry."

"It's okay," I said.

"I guess that would work," Sam said quietly. "It's not too far away."

"Thanks."

"But you wouldn't be ..."

I looked at him.

"In your backyard anymore." Then he blushed.

"Awww," Dell said.

We all laughed and things felt a little better. Sam's hand brushed mine, like he was thinking about holding it, then he pulled away. But it was still sweet.

• • •

Mr. Truelove started the class with our alternative assignment for the year, an assignment that we didn't have to do, he said. Obviously, he got our attention. "This is completely optional. It's a save-your-ass assignment. Although if you didn't quote me on that, I'd appreciate it." He tossed a special little glance toward Troy and Flynn, who only shuffled. "If you need a few extra points at the end of the year, this is the assignment that will make the difference between A or B, pass or fail, depending on what you're shooting for." He looked around the room. "What *are* you shooting for?" He waited as though he was honestly expecting an answer.

We waited until the moment passed for him.

"I was thinking about destiny this weekend." He looked right at me. I looked down at my desk. Somebody had carved "Aieee" into the desk and filled it out in bold, permanent ink. When I looked up, his eyes had moved along.

"And about indecision ... how it can be a fatal flaw." He looked out the window and seemed to drift away on one of the puffy clouds until the growing hum of the class lassoed him back. "Anyway, the assignment is a life resumé. I want you to fill it out as your qualifications come, as they undoubtedly will, in dribs and drabs."

Dell snickered appreciatively, in spite of herself, and I could see her writing down these words. At the end of the year she would have to borrow all my notes because hers would only be special little words and sayings that she found amusing.

"When you're looking for a job, out there in the big, wide world, your employer is going to want to know if you can do the work. Are you qualified? He or she will want to know what you can do. What you are capable of. How you can best serve the job, the company, the role."

A distinct sound of snoring came from somewhere in the room. En masse, the class looked in the direction of Troy and Flynn, but they seemed innocent. Either that or they were excellent ventriloquists.

"Exactly," said Mr. Truelove. "Snoresville."

We all groaned at this. He waited patiently until the room grew silent. In the meantime, Dell sent a note across my desk. It read, HIS SHIRT IS STAPLED SHUT!!! I read it quickly, then folded it and tucked it beneath my binder.

"This is not a resumé that is meant to sell yourself to anyone. It's not even about who you want to be. It's about *how* you want to be. How you want to use the space you're occupying. How you want to serve your life. It's about the hero's adventure. Here's what Mr. Joseph Campbell has to say." He stopped again, but this time there was no snoring, only unnatural quiet. He picked a book up from his desk and began to read. "'We have not even to risk the adventure alone, for the heroes of all time have gone before us. The labyrinth is thoroughly known. We have only to follow the thread of the hero path, and where we had thought to find an abomination, we shall find a god. And where we had thought to slay another, we shall slay ourselves. Where we had thought to travel outward, we will come to the center of our own existence. And where we had thought to be alone, we will be with all the world.'"

Jumpy Kate held up her arm, halfway, cautiously. "Is this psychology?"

He seemed to look through her. "'Strait is the gate, and narrow is the way, which leadeth to life, and few there be who find it.'"

"Um," she said. "Thank you." Ah, Jumpy Kate, so polite. "Should we be writing this down?"

"Write everything down. There. On your life resumé. Everything you go through, everything you experience. Make a list. Then read it over and over and over again."

Dell looked at me and I thought she was going to say, What a wacko, which was what I was thinking. But instead, she mouthed, *I love him.*

What? I mouthed back.

More stealthily than I would have thought possible, Mr. Truelove moved over to my desk and reached beneath my binder, pulling out the note that I thought I had safely spirited away. He read the words and smiled. He lifted up his tie and revealed a shirt that, true enough, was stapled shut. "There's more than one way," he said. He moved over to Dell's desk and returned the note to her. "Nice observation. You can paste that into your life resumé." And then he started talking about BF Skinner and Sigmund Freud and Carl Jung and everything made sense again. The class shook its collective head and started taking notes because this was the stuff we'd be tested on.

• • •

"He's crazy," I said as we stood in the lineup in the cafeteria.

"Oh, no. He's wonderful," Dell said. "I thought you liked him? You were all over him the other day. You abbreviated him."

"I'm over that and I was never all over him. Sheesh."

"I like 'Sheesh.' Very retro," she smiled, still glowing. "But you were."

"Did I tell you that he lives in my dad's building?"

"No way!"

"Why is that so exciting?" The line inched forward. Why did people have such trouble making up their minds over stupid little decisions like what kind of pizza to order?

"I don't know," she admitted. "It just seems mysterious and coincidental and kind of tragic. It is a tragic building."

"I guess."

"Why don't you like him anymore?"

"I never said that."

"You said he was crazy."

"I can like crazy."

"So you do like him."

"I never said that." I groaned. "What are we talking about?" We had reached the head of the line and a lady in a hair net asked what I wanted for lunch. "I don't care," I said without thinking.

"Then get out of the line," said the hair-netted lady.

"Oh, sorry. Hamburger, please. No onions."

She handed me an unadorned hamburger patty on a bun. "Does this look like Burger King?" she said. "Keep moving."

Friendly, I mouthed to Dell, who was busily ordering a lettuce and tomato wrap. "That's all you're having?"

"My hips," she said sadly.

"You don't want hips anymore? How will the top half of your body move? And where will your legs go?"

"Marshall — never mind."

"Never mind what?"

"You're going to go off on me ... like a pistol on a trampoline."

"Pinky swear I will not." We found a table and sat

down. I looked around for Sam, but couldn't see his tousled head.

"Pinky swear you really won't?"

"I just pinky sweared ..."

"Swore. Past tense of swear is swore. Marshall's really into lean. He doesn't even write anymore."

I tried to find the connection. Failed. "Huh?"

"He's a painter now. He thinks colors are more pure than words. That they can express truth more vividly."

"And this applies to hips ...?"

"Everything needs to be pared down to the essentials. Like, do we need the extra body fat when people are starving?"

I took a bite of my hamburger that I'd forgotten to put mustard and ketchup on. "Boy, that Marshall," I said. "He's fun."

"See? I told you ..."

"Tell me about his painting. I want to know." I nodded vigorously and she looked happy again.

As she described his latest passion in painstaking (Technicolor) detail, I looked around for Sam. Still no sign. But Angela was coming our way. As she passed our table, she said, "Hey," and kept on moving toward the group of seniors she'd been absorbed into. She hadn't even had to fill out an application form. It was as if they'd taken one look at her, recognized a fellow vessel of eternal light and said, "Hey, you're one of us! You get over here, you."

"Man, she's beautiful." Dell interrupted her Marshall infomercial long enough to watch Angela reach what she called Those Most Likely to Be Desired. "Does it ever irritate you?"

I remembered what I thought when I saw Angela walk into my house. (Correction: our house. There are no singular possessive pronouns in a blended family.) Perfect. That was the only word that seemed to apply. I thought I'd gotten used to it, but it still startled me sometimes, her beauty. "Nah," I said.

"Liar," Dell laughed. She took a bite of her veggie wrap and looked at me thoughtfully. "So why don't you like Truelove anymore?"

"I do, Dell ... more than the depth and breadth my heart can reach. Is that better?" Stupid Shakespeare. Or was it somebody else? A long-ago English class rankled at me. "Who said that?"

"Elizabeth Barrett Browning. 'I love thee to the depth and breadth and height my soul can reach.'"

"Height? Huh. I never thought about love having height. How tall would love be anyway?"

"Emerson said, 'Thou art to me a delicious torment.' Isn't that wonderful?"

"Don't you ever think that poets have too much time on their hands? Like, go work at the car wash or drive a truck and see how you feel after that?"

She shook her head at me like she suddenly remembered who she was talking to — a girl who enjoys sitcom reruns — and turned back to Marshall news. I tried to block it out. What I suddenly remembered was the look on Mr. Truelove's face as the elevator doors drew shut. Another sad story, and I was sick of those. A delicious torment? Who needed that? Hero's adventure, my big butt.

• • •

"Hey." Sam walked up behind me as I left school. Dell had taken a ride with Marshall. She asked me to come along, but I'd pleaded the need for fresh air.

"Hey yourself. Where were you at lunch?"

"I have darkroom privileges!" he said proudly.

"But you have a darkroom at home."

"Nothing like this. This is the Darth Vader of darkrooms. It's so amazing, I can't tell you."

"Like it's a secret?"

He smiled. I melted. And then he morphed into cute/hot boy and I panicked. I shook my head quickly, back and forth, so I'd feel normal again. So the pieces of my brain would stop drifting apart and join together again the way they were supposed to.

"What's wrong with you?"

"Nothing. Tell me about the amazing, secret darkroom."

"No. We need to talk about our first date."

"How was it?" My stomach suddenly clenched into a big, tight, hard ball of tight hardness. (Where was Dell when I needed a word?)

"No." He shook his blond hair. His face split in two with a big grin just the way it did when he showed me his first camera. He was already breaking my heart. "We haven't had it yet."

My brain evaporated. "I know."

"I know you know. Here's the thing," he said. He started walking down the sidewalk. I moved along beside him, grateful to have something to occupy the now empty space in my head. Walking. I could do that. Of course I could do that.

"What's the thing?"

"It has to be something good."

"Okay."

"Nothing lame like dinner or a movie or bowling."

"No bowling?"

"You want to go bowling?"

"I'm just not sure I want it off the list."

"There's a list?" he asked. "Okay, it's back on the list. But not the A list."

"So it'll be on the B list?"

"Sure."

"Whew."

He smiled again. I wished he would stop doing that. Every time, things went fuzzy. He had no idea how many of my brain cells he was killing when he smiled. "Paint ball."

"Paint ball?" Okay, maybe I had one or two brain cells left. "You want to shoot me? On our first date?"

"You're right."

"We'll put it on the B list."

"How about laser tag?"

"Hmm."

"B list?"

"No, I shouldn't be in charge of the list, Sam. I don't want to be in charge. Laser tag will be fun."

"No. That was lame. I'm lame."

"You're not lame."

He tried to smile, but he couldn't. I remembered the message on my desk, that dark, forboding message: *Aieee*. Maybe I'd already wrecked it? Maybe that would be my first entry on my life resumé. Date wrecker.

"We could do dinner, I guess," he finally said.

"I like to eat. I love eating!"

"Okay. Saturday night. Eating."

"Definitely A list."

When we got to the point where our two houses abut, I said, "So, I'm home."

There was a weird, unfamiliar, awkward pause wherein I realized that an incredibly awkward moment can always become more awkward. "I'm looking forward to eating," I said.

"Me, too," he said.

"Well, bye."

"Bye."

As I entered my house I noticed that my dad was sitting on the couch next to my mother. There's always more awkward.

Chapter Eight

I marched into the room. "Okay, we need to talk," I said before either one of them got a chance to say it. They seemed a little surprised. This was good. I was counting on the element of surprise. "I'm over it. I'm willing to move on. In the meantime ... life goes on. Lots of homework to do. Just wanted to let you know that I'm willing to let bygones be bygones." I delivered my speech and almost made it out of the room. I was so close. My foot was actually across the threshold when Dad's voice drew me back.

"Nice try, kiddo."

I dragged myself to the big overstuffed chair, flopped into it and stared into space.

Mom perched forward on the couch. "I think we've gotten our wires crossed."

I could not prevent my groan. If I could have saved the entire world from total doom, I could not have stopped that groan.

Then the door opened and Angela floated in. Maybe it was all the yoga she'd been doing, but she seemed to pick up the negative vibe. She passed through the room quickly.

"Jes, just hear us out," Dad said.

I forced a smile. "Us?" I said. "Which 'us' is that? I'm sorry, I'm lost. I've been having a pronoun crisis. I — "

"Enough, Jes. Enough." My mother's voice was shaking. Instantly, she composed herself. "Your father and I have cleared up the misunderstanding about you living with him."

"Didn't you say that I could live with you?" I said.

"In theory, of course ..."

"Oh, *in theory*. See, didn't know that. My mistake. I thought you meant it."

"I did mean it," he said. "I do mean it." Now he looked helpless, which was only slightly less gross than looking vulnerable. "I didn't know *you* meant it." His voice trailed away.

My mom shook her head. "Thank you, Steven. That was helpful."

"Elli, I just want her to know that I'm here for her, okay?"

Holy Moses in the Desert, I'd turned into Hamlet, Sr., making unreasonable requests, causing all manner of problems when I should have kept my big fat ghost trap shut. Of all the things I didn't want, I didn't want my parents fighting again. "I'm sorry, I'm sorry," I said. What was wrong with my voice? Was I five years old? My eyes were burning, but I wouldn't cry. I had to contort my face into a pretty unattractive position to pull this off, but I think I did. God, misery was humiliating. "I thought it would be a good solution."

Then my mom's face crumpled and I thought she was going to cry, but she didn't. Her voice, instead, went rigid with anger. "You are not a problem to be solved. You are my daughter and you are going to live here. Your father has offered to renovate the house. That is a reasonable solution. We are all going to be very, very, very reasonable. Is that understood? And now I need to throw up."

My dad and I looked at each other as she left the room.

"Yeah," he said. "That went well. This is gonna work." He kissed my head and he, too, left the room.

• • •

"So your mom was quite masterful?" said Dell.

"Oh yeah. She was something."

"But you get a new room."

"Yep. That's ... something." I was too tired to find a new word.

"Hold out for a bay window. Or a balcony. A balcony would be cool. Sam could climb up the trellis. Very Romeo and Juliet." I listened as Dell transformed my life into romance. Sometimes she just didn't get it. And then she switched to the Marshall channel, which was preferable. As she talked, it occurred to me that some people went looking for tragedy while others had it thrust upon them. I wondered, again, why this was.

After I got off the phone, I pulled a new notebook and a black marker out of my backpack. In bloated letters, I wrote "LIFE RESUMÉ." Under that I scrawled, "Misery."

• • •

Dinner was strained. Cal had gone for a ride with his riding buddies. (Imagine a middle-aged man in tights, and then imagine seven or eight of them. There you go. Now try to get rid of the image.) Angela grazed on her raw foods while Mom and I shared a pizza, the only thing that she could keep down these days.

"Maybe the baby's Italian," Angela suggested. "I think Cal has some Italian blood in him somewhere." It was kind of weird to hear her call him Cal, but she'd given up the "Dad." It did make things simpler for general identification purposes. No more *Your dad and Cal, I mean, Dad and Jes's dad, etc.*

"I didn't know that," said Mom politely. Her face was pale.

"So when does this whole puking phase end?" I asked.

"Usually after the first trimester, but sometimes it just keeps going." She put down her first piece of pizza as if she'd already had enough.

"You know, Elli, you really should be eating more vegetables. And drinking milk, although I'm not sure that cow milk is the best way to go. How do you feel about soy?"

"I, well, I have no opinion about soy." She rubbed her temples with her fingers. She kept rubbing as Angela talked about vitamins and some stupid soothing mantra that was supposed to provide a tranquil haven for the embryo and blah blah blah.

When it seemed she would never stop, I interrupted. "Are you okay, Mom? You don't look very good."

"I've got a bit of a headache. I think I'll go upstairs and rest."

"Do you want a cup of tea?" Angela said.

She tried to smile, but that looked painful. "That would be nice," she said as she left the room.

Angela started to get up, but I stopped her. "I'll do it."

"I don't mind."

"I'll do it," I said, more forcefully than I intended.

"Fine. Just make sure it's chamomile. If her blood pressure is elevated, she shouldn't have the caffeine. At her age ..."

"Got it."

"I just ..." She shook her head. "I'm going to the gym. I'll see you later."

I cleaned up the kitchen while I waited for the kettle to boil. I was grateful that she'd left, although it did cross my mind that she could have at least offered to help clean up. Oh well. Even perfection required maintenance, it seemed. It also crossed my mind that

I was going to have to wise up about prenatal matters unless I wanted to listen to Expert Angela for the next six months.

When the tea was ready, I took it upstairs, but my mother was asleep. I put it on the nightstand and watched her. Her forehead wasn't furrowed anymore and she was breathing evenly, but she still looked tired.

• • •

Instead of doing homework, I spent the evening researching all things baby. Apparently this little baby whatsit had been spending the first months of its — okay, his — life developing at super speed. This is how the Internet article put it anyway. Within half an hour of fertilization — the average lengh of a sitcom — the fertilized egg "begins dividing at a furious rate while traveling down the Fallopian tube to the uterus where it implants itself in the wall." And that was only the first half hour! After that it was a constant thrum of activity as he cleverly developed cells, a rudimentary brain, the beginning of arms and legs and eyes, nose and ears. It was dizzying. By now he'd already figured out how to move his head, body and limbs and respond to tactile stimulation. The picture was disgusting, something between a rodent and an alien, but you had to admire the progress he'd made, although clearly not in the personal-looks department. I couldn't help but think that maybe I had something to learn from my little brother.

Little brother. The two words came out of nowhere

or, maybe, from somewhere between fertilization and the beginnings of a rudimentary brain, but still they did nothing for me. The words meant nothing.

• • •

I must have fallen asleep because otherwise there was no explaining the image in my head of a baby with a ginormous head wearing spandex shorts sitting in the lotus position singing "We All Live in a Yellow Submarine." But I was awake now and there was a definite humming noise, which could have been the sound of a spaceship. I was considering the possibility of alien abduction when I recognized the noise of the blow drier, pretty much a constant since Angela had moved in.

I staggered to the bathroom under the weight of my nap hangover and found Angela there, smoothing her already shimmery mane of hair.

"Hey," I said.

"Do you need the bathroom? I'm almost done."

"No, it's okay. I just need a glass of water."

"No problem. I'll get out of your way."

"You're not in my way," I said testily. I leaned over, turned on the tap and filled a glass. I avoided my reflection. Who needed that? "There. Done."

Angela turned off the drier, folded up the cord and placed it neatly away, the way she always did. "I was just trying to help."

Maybe it was the nap, but I had no idea what she was talking about.

"Before. At dinner. I mean, I know it's none of my business, okay? I know that. I just — " She shrugged. "I know that."

I thought about following her to her room, but she closed her door behind her. Almost immediately the sound of her music haunted the hallway.

I went to my room and opened the notebook. I looked at the word "misery" for a long time. I tried to think of something else, something more positive, but I was stuck. I thought about crossing it out, at least, but I didn't. In the end, all I could do was close the book.

Chapter Nine

I woke up the next morning to the sight of my dad in my room. It was a sight that was both familiar and unfamiliar. I felt the old knot. I closed my eyes, convinced that I was still dreaming. I tried to shift the dreamscape to something less disturbing: my date with Sam later that night. Aieee. The knot tightened.

"Sorry for waking you up."

I popped one eye open. Nope, not a dream. "Dad. What are you doing?"

"Well, I tried to wait until you woke up, but it's past noon! Boy, can you sleep."

"I am an excellent sleeper," I said. I yawned and pulled myself up on my elbows. Maybe I would put that on my life resumé: excellent sleeper. "Again, what are you doing?"

"Measuring."

"Oh." I yawned again. "What?"

"The room, you silly twit."

It all came back to me. The big black cloud in the living room, my mother's tired face, my dad's defeat. All of it. "You don't have to do that, Dad. I'm over it.

Seriously. I'll move in with Angela and I'll learn to love sitar music. We'll all do deep belly cleanses in perfect harmony."

"I know. I heard the music when I came in. And the vacuum cleaner. Boy, she's a tidy one, isn't she?"

"Uh-huh."

He sat on the corner of my bed and looked around the room. I knew he was remembering: night feedings, bedtime stories, puppet games with socks. "It's time to pull down a few old walls, Funny Face. Why don't you go downstairs and get some breakfast. I won't be long."

"Do you want anything?"

"A cup of joe?"

I laughed. "That's coffee in English, right?"

"Sweet and white," he said over his shoulder. He was already kneeling on the floor, taking measurements and writing them down. Also familiar. Measuring and reading were his two favorite pastimes.

I wrapped myself in my quilt. "Sounds like somebody's spending too much time at the diner." I stumbled down the stairs and into the kitchen. Angela and Mom were reading the paper while Cal flipped pancakes. Every Saturday, Cal made pancakes. I think it was the only thing he knew how to cook. But they were good pancakes, I reminded myself. "Hey," I said.

"Good morning," Mom smiled. She looked rested and her cheeks were pink again. "Did you see your dad?"

"Hard to miss." I slumped down on a chair and rested my head comfortably on the table. "The man loves to measure."

Her laugh was a nice sound. "That he does."

"Pancakes?" Cal said. He sounded jolly but tense. Like Santa on the day before Christmas.

"No, thanks. Just some coffee."

"When did you start drinking coffee?" Mom asked.

"Not for me. For Dad."

"Two sugars and lots of cream." she said, returning to her paper. "I don't know how he drinks it like that."

I heard a soft thud as a steaming mug of coffee was put in front of me. I looked up. Cal was standing beside me with the spatula in his hand. From my position, he looked like some weird king holding a rubber scepter. A king in an apron. "Thanks." My mother took the coffee and added the sugar and cream, stirred it, then slid it back to me. Cal watched her the whole time.

"Are you sure you don't want any pancakes? I added blueberries," he said. Now, on top of the tense sound in his voice, there was a hint of pleading. Oh, great. One more vulnerable parent. I refused to look into his eyes. A girl had to draw the line somewhere.

"Maybe later," I said. I took the coffee and shuffled out of the room with my quilt still draped around me. Cal followed me, still grasping his scepter.

"Jes, hold on."

I stopped mid-staircase and sat down. "Yes?"

"I just wanted to say something that I probably should have said the other day." Mayday, mayday. "The other day? When your mother and I told you about the baby?"

"Uh-huh."

"I'm sorry that I raised my voice. I should have known better."

I knew what was coming. He was going to recite a passage from the stepfather manual. Could I cut him off politely? Could I? "That's okay, Cal. These are trying times."

He smiled a little. I reminded myself that he had a nice smile, kind of shy. "You're right." He put his hand up to his face. He must have forgotten that he was holding the spatula, at least until he felt the batter. "It's just that I know better. I know it's too soon for any kind of authoritative parental intervention on my part."

Oh. My. I couldn't stop my smile so I pointed to his forehead. "You have a little, er ... batter."

"Thanks." He swiped, but only succeeded in smearing the glob. I quickly pinched myself in order to deflect an inappropriate stepchild exchange.

"It's really important, crucial, to avoid jumping in too soon to fix things. So, I'm sorry for that."

For a second there was a sliver of silence when I could nod and walk away. And then I said, "Fix me? I didn't know I was broken." Ah, so close.

He opened his mouth, but obviously his inner shut-up mechanism was more advanced than mine. He walked back into the kitchen.

I dropped off the coffee, snuck back down the stairs (Dell would say "sneaked") and found my way to a patch of sun in the backyard. I grabbed the basketball and hurled it over the fence into Sam's backyard. Sure enough, within seconds, it came hurtling back, almost nailing me. I waited for the rhodo bush to move; it hid the break in the fence that no one had ever fixed. Danny's bright blond head, still streaked a thousand enviable shades of yellow from the summer sun, poked through. "You want Sam?"

"Yep."

"I'll get him."

I heard him run through the yard, screaming for all the neighbors to hear. "Sam, Jes wants you." I could hear Henry's voice from inside the house. "She wants you baaad." Maybe next time I'd use the telephone.

Soon, Sam pushed his way past the bush with his camera dangling from his neck. "You bounced?"

"Hey." I was suddenly perfectly happy.

He pulled up a lawn chair and sat beside me. His glance took in the quilt. "I see you're dressed for our date."

His words brought me back to The New Reality.

He wasn't just my friend anymore; he was outside of that comfortable place. "You didn't tell me where we were going, so I decided ..." But I couldn't think of anything clever. My voice faded away.

"You okay?"

"I'm just tired. What were you doing?" I pointed to his camera with a blanketed hand. "Oh, duh."

"My mom's making jam. Every year it's the same. Henry starts eating all the berries and then throwing them at Danny; they start fighting, so my dad starts yelling and my mom says she never gets any peace ever — is a little peace too much to ask? — and, well, somebody has to record it for posterity."

"And that's your job?"

"As the eldest." He puffed his chest out proudly. "Besides, nobody ever hits the guy with the camera, right?"

"In a war?"

He shrugged. "It's more of a skirmish. No fatalities yet."

I smiled and leaned back to catch the sun on my face. It felt good. And then I heard a click of the shutter. "Sam," I whined, pulling the blanket over my head. "I look awful."

"You look cute." He snapped again.

"Stop it."

"Jeez, you're cranky in the morning."

"I am not," I said, in a muffled blanket voice. "And it's not morning."

A crash and then a bellow from Sam's dad, Geoff, whose bark was far worse than his bite. I heard Sam get out of the chair. "Duty calls. I'll pick you up at six o'clock, okay? Lose the blanket."

I poked my head out to say good-bye and noticed that he was waving to my house. That was weird. I turned and saw my dad's face in my window.

"Your dad's here?"

"Don't ask."

• • •

Seeing that the blanket option had been taken away, I spent most of the afternoon rooting through my closet figuring out what to wear. I started with the dress I'd worn to my mother's wedding. It was a little shorter, but it still looked good. At least, I thought it did, but my mirror was covered with the blanket so I had no real way of knowing. Yes, I could have taken the blanket off, but my stubborn little soccer voice was still chirping, *Why should I?* And I had no good answer.

Anyway, we weren't going to a prom. I took it off and moved on to pants and shirts and skirts and tops and combinations of all of the above. At one point I had tried on everything I owned. With Keds or without? Sandals, maybe. It was still summer-ish. I'd have to put nail polish on my toes. Screw that. I considered calling Sam to say that we needed to cancel the whole thing, but then I'd have to tell him I have nothing to wear, and that would be a cliché. I called Dell instead.

She arrived at three o'clock with her arms full of clothes. She has five inches on me, so most things hung on me like a kid playing dress-up, but I appreciated the thought.

"What do you think of that?" she asked, after convincing me to try on a bright orange halter top.

"I don't know. What do you think?"

"Well, look in the mirror." She started to take the blanket away.

"Stop!" I yelled.

"What?" She jumped.

"It's cracked," I lied. "It's bad luck."

Dell was very superstitious. "Oh, thanks. Let's go to the bathroom."

"Why? You have eyes. How does it look?"

"Well, I think it looks fine, oh weird one. Don't you want to see?"

"I have no need."

She laughed. "How nice for you." There was a knock at the door. "Come in," she called, still laughing.

Angela opened the door and Dell's smile fizzled. Until that cornfield kiss, she and Angela had gotten pretty tight, but she had vowed never to get over Angela's betrayal.

"Hi, Dell," Angela said pleasantly. Dell muttered hello and backed into the corner. "Your mom's going to the grocery store," she said to me, "and she wants to know if you need anything."

"Six more inches."

"I'll let her know." She looked around the room and shook her head. "I don't know how you can even breathe in here," she said in wonder. I considered telling her to *feng shui* herself, and then she added, "Orange is so not your color."

Orange *was* the color of Dell's face, I noticed, once the door closed. "The nerve, the gall, the unmitigated impudence ..."

"Okay, have your stroke on your own time. I need clothes." I looked at my watch. "Aieee, it's almost five o'clock!"

The door opened again. This time Angela walked straight in. A couple of pieces of clothing were draped neatly over her arm. "Here, try these on."

"We're doing fine," Dell said with her nose in the air. Her posture always improved when Angela was around. Actually, Angela had that effect on everybody. "We don't need your help."

Angela sighed. "Listen, I'm sorry about what happened with Marshall, okay? Really, I am."

Dell looked away.

"Fine." Angela turned to me. "But you? You need my help."

"Thanks, but we're not the same size," I said, stating the painfully obvious. "In case you hadn't noticed."

"Give me some credit. The skirt is short on me and it has an elastic waist. It's going to fall just above your knees and it's going to look amazing because you have great calves and pretty ankles. The pink camisole is going to work with your complexion; it'll bring out the color of your eyes, which are spectacular, by the way. It's also constructed in such a way that will give you some nice cleavage ... nothing slutty, just nice."

"She doesn't need help there," said Dell, in what was possibly the boldest lie of the day.

"I'm not saying she does," Angela said patiently. "It'll just give her a pretty décolletage."

Dell gasped and I knew it was word envy. I, of course, had never heard the word before, but I was pretty good at piecing things together. "Thanks," I said meekly.

"The sweater is in case it gets cool. Make sure you have the camisole peeking out a little at the bottom."

Dell snorted. "Peeking?"

We both looked at her.

"I'm just saying, can a camisole peek? Can it really? I think that's called anthromorphizing the shirt."

"Anthro-po-morphizing, actually. But I think you're clear on the concept, aren't you, Jes?"

I nodded.

"You're on your own for shoes," Angela continued, "because I have monster feet. I suggest sandals. I'd look through your closet, but the thought honestly terrifies me." And then she left.

I tried on the outfit while Dell muttered, "Décolletage, my big butt. And I knew it was anthropomorphize ..."

"Focus," I said, pointing to myself.

Dell just stared. "She's a witch," she finally said.

"That bad?" I started to pull the skirt off.

"No." Her shoulders slumped. "You look amazing."

• • •

Sam's reaction to my outfit was not quite as eloquent.

"Wow," he said. "You look, like, really, like ... you do."

I was about to respond when I noticed Amber standing behind Sam on the front stairs. "You brought your mother?"

Sam twisted around. "M-o-o-om. I told you to stay home."

"I am here to see Elli. Is that all right? Am I allowed to visit my friend?" She brushed past me and whispered, "Oh, Sweetie. You look beautiful."

"Doesn't she?" Mom said from behind me.

I grabbed Sam's arm. "We gotta make a break for it."

"Have a good time," the two mothers chimed as we walked to the sidewalk in record speed.

"She wanted to bring the camera," Sam said, disgusted.

"A camera? Can you imagine that?" I laughed.

He looked sheepish. "Whatever. Listen," he said, suddenly sounding very businesslike. "We can take the Number Two bus to Luigi's. It'll only take about twenty minutes. My mother offered to drive us, but I said I'd rather impale myself on a rusty sword."

"And then you'd need a tetanus shot ..."

"Plus hospital food sucks ..."

"So how much fun would that be?" I concluded. I thought to myself that this whole thing was so much easier than I imagined it would be and how silly I was to worry. That I was with Sam. Sam! My friend since forever — and how perfect this all was and the sky was just the right color of orange and pink (probably matching my lovely complexion). And then he held my hand and it seemed kind of weird, like it wasn't really us, but I didn't mind at first, in fact I liked it, but then I did mind it. Or at least I minded that I didn't mind because it didn't feel like us. *That's* what I really minded. What next? Where would it end?

Stop it, I told myself sternly. I knew I wasn't thinking straight. But the whole skin-on-skin contact had the same effect as his smile and I could feel my brain cells trickling out, like Hansel dropping bread crumbs. I couldn't think of a thing to say so we just walked, glued together by our sticky hands. When we got to the bus stop it seemed we both didn't quite understand the finer points of hand-holding. When did you drop the hand? Was it considered rude to be the first one to let go? Would this be a huge breach of dating protocol? Were we to be glued together, both of us shuffling along, for life? Buried in one big casket because nobody let go? So much for happily ever after.

Miserably, we waited for the bus. Then Sam had a stroke of genius and decided to look at the bus schedule, even though we both knew darned well that it would come when it came and not a moment before. Still, he had to let go of my hand and I could breathe again. "So, Luigi's, eh?"

"Is that okay? We could go somewhere else? How about Earl's or Cactus Club?" He continued to rattle off the names of every single restaurant in town while I shook my head like I'd developed some life-threatening palsy.

"No, no, Luigi's sounds great. It's just what I imagined."

"You imagined? What did you imagine?" He sounded scared. Why was he scared?

"Nothing."

Now he looked confused. "But you said."

"Oh, you know me. I'm always saying stuff."

He really looked like he wanted this to make sense. Fortunately the bus came and we climbed aboard. People smiled as we took our seats and I realized that we totally looked like we were on a date. For the first time I noticed what he was wearing. A blue blazer, new jeans and a pink shirt with a green stripe. I'd seen the exact outfit at American Eagle. Oh, so cute. He was breaking my heart again. I pulled my sweater close around my décolletage.

• • •

I'd really like to say that things went better after that. I'd like to say that we both loosened up and fell back into being ourselves. That's the ending I'd like to report. The falling was there, but it was more like dream-falling where you thought, Wake up, already, before you hit the rocks.

By the time the pasta arrived in the hands of a guy named Benny, we'd run out of ways to say that the weather was unseasonably warm. Sam had ordered tortellini and I had decided on the lasagna. While we waited for the food to cool down, we talked about the amazing invention of pasta. Who decided that flour and water could ever be anything but paste? This line of conversation held some promise, but we both ran out of things to say after I noticed that if you changed the "e" in "paste" to an "a" you had "pasta" and Sam said, "Ah." After that, we ate in silence until every scrap of food was gone.

"Well," Sam said as the dishes were cleared away by Benny. "What do you want to do now?"

"I don't believe in teenage sex," I declared.

He looked exactly the way he had when I accidentally shot him with his BB gun when we were ten. "I was thinking, maybe, dessert."

We were deadly quiet on the bus ride home — mere corpses of our former selves. Rigor mortis had set in. No war, no pestilence, no calamity could compare with my monumental blurtation. Finally, we walked the longest mile back to our houses, where we both morphed back to our own selves as we stood in front of my gate. We sighed and looked at each other, utterly exhausted.

Sam ran his hand through his hair so that it stood straight up. (He'd used more gel than needed.) "Man, that was gruesome."

"No kidding."

"So this is probably a bad idea."

"Would never have worked."

"We're good at being friends."

"We are the best at that," I said.

"Okay."

"Okay."

"See you tomorrow?" he said.

"You know where I live."

I climbed my stairs with the weight of the world lifted off of me. I wasn't cut out for romance; that was clear. And how smart were we to figure this out before we'd sliced each other's hearts into little pieces? So smart. Best thing ever.

• • •

I went to Angela's room the next morning to return her clothes. She wasn't there. I heard the whir of the blow drier. Of course. I knocked on the bathroom door. "I'm almost done," she said.

"I just wanted to tell you that I returned your clothes. And thanks."

She opened the door. "No problem. How did it go?"

I leaned against the doorjamb. "Oh, you know."

"Not good?"

"Nah, but it's better this way. We're better at friends."

She shrugged and returned to her hair. For some

reason my shoulder was stuck to the door. I was hypnotized by how she looked in the mirror. Perfect. I know it seems dumb, but I couldn't see her and not see perfection. I knew better, obviously, since that day she lied about sticking the necklace she stole in my backpack. Later, when she decided to live with us, she told me about her wacko mother who'd said she hadn't wanted her, so I knew her life hadn't been perfect. Even so, her face bore no evidence of this. Instead, she was walking proof of how you could look if all the gods of beauty had a party, got drunk and decided to come up with something *really* spectacular. Looking in the mirror, I wondered if beauty was a lie. Or maybe just a fib. Either way, not the whole truth.

"What are you looking at?" she said. She didn't sound mad, just curious.

"You're just really beautiful."

Angela smiled like she'd heard it before. Dell would hate the smile because she would think it was conceited.

"Oh, her?" Angela said, looking in the mirror. "She's not real. She's just a reflection. A ... version." Then her smile changed, became hard. "But she *is* pretty hot, I'll give you that."

Wintertime

Chapter Ten

My mother's belly was now the size of a small pumpkin. Fetal formation is usually described in terms of fruit, but I was going with a vegetable motif. Unless pumpkin was a fruit? Crap. Well, whatever you wanted to compare it to, it was growing.

The rest of us were the same size. That's not quite true either. Crap. Angela was growing more and more taut, as if willing every muscle, tendon, sinew and synapse to conform to yogic perfection; Cal was as lean as a whippet from all the miles he covered on his bike; my dad, in his workman shirts, seemed burlier than usual with all his wall-tearing-down; and even Dell, who wasn't part of the family, strictly speaking, was growing thinner.

I suspected that Dell's skinniness had something to do with Marshall, but I was trying to be positive about him since he wasn't going anywhere. Dell had almost gotten over the fact that Sam and I weren't either. Almost. Every once in a while she still felt the need to bring up my blurtation.

Like yesterday. We were at the grocery store for my mother, who suddenly needed Chinese mandarin oranges. Not Japanese or Taiwanese or Korean, and not any other citrus fruit from any other country. Only Chinese mandarins would do. (Apparently young Sir Whatsit's tastes are very specific.) I had asked a guy in the produce department where the oranges were. "Right over there," he pointed out, friendly enough, smiling in a nice produce-guy way.

"Thanks," I said in a nice produce-shopper way.

Dell was suddenly at my side. "She doesn't believe in teenage sex."

I blushed crimson all the way past the checkout line and into the parking lot, where I asked her why, again, we were friends.

"I am trying to help you get over the need to say every little thing that pops into your head. It's aversion therapy."

"Thanks," I said. "I think I'm over it."

"We'll see," she grumbled. She said she was ticked off that things hadn't worked out between Sam and me — we were "meant to be together." But I suspected — and I told her — that she wanted me to be a couple so that me/we could hang out with her and Marshall. "You want me to be a we," was how I put it.

"Is that so wrong?" she said, a little bit sadly.

I said it wasn't and I thought that the way she was sad about the stupidest things was one of the things that I loved about her. But it's not what you say to a girlfriend — I don't know why.

That's the thing, though — why does anybody love anybody? It couldn't just be a feeling, because feelings change. Instinct? Maybe. But that seemed so cold. Like animals. Like there was no other choice and it all boiled down to a basic need, like eating or drinking or survival. Too caveman. But I didn't get Dell's idea of love, that was for sure. Maybe I did, once upon a time, but all that romantic stuff seemed dangerous, like running with scissors. Sure it seems like a great idea when you're a kid. But eventually you grow up and you realize that it's a bad idea. (Possibly just after you've stuck the sharp end through your eyeball.) Love seemed very dangerous and it seemed to make people stupid. Lately I've even been wondering if maybe all the poets and philosophers and movie makers weren't just trying to make a buck or two on our collective stupidity. Sell a few sappy stories, buy a pool. Maybe we were all being duped. Bottom line: maybe a person *could* live without love. And maybe we'd all get a lot more done.

The only thing that screwed up this otherwise sound theory was that sometimes — just rarely — I still wondered what Sam's lips would feel like.

• • •

On the last day of school before Christmas vacation I waited for Dell outside her house. Sam had gone early, the way he did more and more these days. He said it was because of his duties as class photographer.

I wondered if he was trying to avoid me.

"Hi," she said, flying down her walkway, pulling her heavy jacket around her diminishing frame. "Sorry I'm late."

"No problem."

She pulled her coat tighter around her even though it wasn't that cold.

"How much do you weigh now?" I said.

"I thought you were over the blurting-out of things?"

"I'm working on it. You just look so thin. Good," I added quickly, "but thin. Is Marshall still boycotting hips?"

"I love him. I told him last night."

"Whoa. Talk about your major blurtation."

"But it's true."

"So is the fact that the earth is round."

"That's illogical."

"You caught me off guard."

"Or maybe it isn't? Maybe you're actually saying that my love for Marshall is as self-evident as the earth being round."

"Or maybe you caught me off guard," I said. "Let's go back to where you said you told Marshall you love him."

"It was so romantic."

My intestines squeezed together like an accordion; I could practically hear the music. (There's a pretty picture.)

"We were at his house, making out and such ... "

"And such?"

She smiled in a knowledgeable/wistful kind of way. Knowledgeable because she knew way more than I did about these matters and wistful because she knew way more than I did about these matters. "Well, not *and such* and such, if you know what I mean. But *and such* as in more than usual. Et al, as the Latins would say."

"Ah, the Latins. I wish I understood that," I finally said.

"He knows that I want to wait, okay?"

"Okay." I understood this. "Is he okay with that?"

"Oh, yeah. He totally gets me, Jes. When we're together it's like he's the only one in the world who knows who I really am."

This hurt, but I didn't say. "So when did the whole love thing come up?"

She laughed merrily and blushed so that even the tips of her ears went red. I knew we'd entered new territory: the land of *and such*. "He just said that sometimes he didn't know if he could stand loving me so much." She waited for me to insert a comment, but what could I say? My first thought was that it sounded like he was horny, and I was not going to blurt that out.

"So what did you say?" I asked instead.

Dell sighed. "That I loved him. And I do — I really do."

"How does it feel?" I didn't expect this question from myself, but her eyes were so shiny and she looked, well, "transformed" seemed too strong, but she looked different.

"Like absolutely nothing else in the world. It's completely new. Like it was God's best idea yet."

Oh dear, I thought.

"I was at the bus stop on the way home and I saw these old people — like, ancient — getting onto the bus. A young guy was helping them and he was so sweet. He held their hands and guided them up the stairs; he moved so carefully and slowly, the way they were moving. And I thought it was all the same. Love, you know? It's all the same."

She looked so happy. Why was it breaking my heart? Why was everything breaking my heart these days? I needed a new phrase. My heart was cracking like a mirror and, in each of the hundred reflections, all I could see was Dell at the bus stop alone. "Was Marshall there with you? Waiting for the bus?" I asked, just in case I was wrong.

"No," she said, as if it hadn't even occurred to her.

• • •

Truelove was late. I sat at my desk thinking about what this statement could mean because Dell was daydreaming and the rest of the class was mesmerized by Troy and Flynn's amazing pencil-up-the-nose-look-I'm-a-walrus trick.

I was thinking that maybe *Truelove was late* could

mean not having a boyfriend until a person was too old to care, or it could mean a late period. And that made me think of Dell's *and such*. Dell could be swept off her feet so easily — like a dust bunny, really. I was wandering down this particularly worrisome road when Truelove showed up.

Sometimes, lately, I preferred to think of him as George. Especially since my dad had gotten to know him. Wouldn't you know that my father would say that his daughter was in George's psychology class, and wasn't that the biggest coincidence ever? My dad said that George had *brightened* and, if that wasn't corny enough, added that George seemed *quite taken with you*.

My bowels actually clenched when he said this, but he wasn't finished. "Especially your take on *Hamlet*."

"I don't have a take on *Hamlet*," I protested. I hate it when teachers — or anybody, for that matter — overestimate me. "Zero take on *Hamlet*. Sub-zero."

My dad refused to be unimpressed and added that George was going through a divorce so I should go easy on him. (I promised I'd cancel my plans to egg his car.) Then he said that he might go out for a beer with George sometime. Was I okay with that? I said it was fine, but I said it with a huge sigh, which my dad skipped past, which made me feel a little ignored.

Anyway, Truelove did not simply enter the room; Truelove stumbled into the room.

"Walk much?" said clever Troy.

I waited for his courtly leave-the-room gesture, but Truelove only gave him the same hapless look I'd seen that day the elevator door closed and I had a feeling that something was about to go horribly wrong.

"Today is the last day before Christmas break," he said precisely. "Traditionally it is a time of good cheer and gift giving and love. 'Love, love, love. All you need is love.'" He glanced around the room; I checked out the surface of my desk to see if "Aieee" was still there. Please don't sing, please don't sing is what I was thinking. "Today we will discuss the psychology of love."

Jumpy Kate raised a bold arm. "Is this in the textbook?"

"It should be," he said.

"Will we be tested on it?"

"Most definitely," he said. "Numerous times."

I retraced the letters so the "Aieee" grew even more pronounced. Out of the corner of my eye I could see that Dell was listening intently—head thrust out, serious cheek chewing. Her pencil moved smoothly as she plucked out words that appealed, that sounded a special note that only she could hear; all the while she watched Truelove's face to match up the words with his expression or some other telling detail that she would put in brackets. At the end of the class she would have something like a poem; at the end of the term I'd get a phone call for something like sentences and paragraphs and facts.

Truelove talked about the troubadours of the twelfth century and how they were the singers of love. How they had cracked open the surface of their world. I took notes because everyone else was and I didn't want to get left behind if there was a test, but I didn't think there would be. There was something a little off about the way he looked, and that was saying something for a guy who stapled his shirts shut and thought shaving was for special occasions. It was like he'd gone blurry, out of focus, like he was reciting the things he was saying, but not from a textbook.

The troubadours, those zany singers of love, he said, celebrated life directly through the experience of love. They saw love as a force, but not a power. It was a force that opened the heart to the sad, bitter-sweet melody of being. It intertwined one's anguish and one's joy. Their motive, he said, was to sublimate life into a spiritual plane of existence.

At this point, Jumpy Kate asked if I knew how to spell "sublimate." I asked her why she didn't ask Dell, the resident spelling-bee champion for four years in a row in elementary school, but she just jerked her head in Dell's direction. Sure enough, Dell was spellbound. (Ironic, I thought, that I couldn't share this fabulous wordplay with Dell, for obvious reasons.) She was hooked. It sounded like hooey to me.

By now Truelove had moved on to the Round Table and knights and kings and holy grails and I stopped taking notes for serious because I suddenly remembered where I'd seen the look. It was the look of the Holy Tangent, the big one-eighty desperate parents take when they're trying to explain something inexplicable. (In my parents' case I witnessed it during the now-famous discussion of love as a melting ice-cream sundae. Or was that marriage?)

Romantic legends, Truelove said, were a search for the reuniting of what had been divided, the peace that comes from joining. The best we can do is lean toward the light that comes from compassion with suffering from understanding the other person. (Wow, I thought, that sounded like fun.) The romance is a divine visitation, he said. Pain, he said, growing red in his stubbled face. The pain of love is the pain of life.

Thank God and all the saints and angels for Jumpy Kate, who could stand it no longer. "Is this really going to be on a test?" she asked suspiciously.

Truelove barely seemed to register the question, but he did stop talking. For at least a minute, maybe two, he just stood there. I thought he was going to start crying. Instead he said, "Put it on your life resumé." Then he left the room.

I waved to Dell, planning to say, "Hooey," because I liked the word and I thought she would too, but she was still in a trance. I threw my eraser at her. When she turned, her eyes were wet with tears. "Oh, crap," I said instead.

"Did you hear what he said about the wasteland?"

I looked down at my notes. "Nope."

"He said it's a land where everybody lives an inauthentic life, doing as other people do, doing as you're told, with no courage to live your own life."

"Wow," I said, impressed. "You wrote down an entire complex sentence?"

"That's me, Jes." Two tears trailed down her cheeks like perfect beads. I knew I'd felt trouble in the air.

• • •

On the way home I asked her about the waterworks. It was too soon to joke, as I discovered when she welled up again.

"My parents want me to break up with Marshall."

"What?"

"They think we're spending too much time together."

You are, I thought.

"That he has too much of an influence on me."

He does, I thought.

"That he doesn't really appreciate me and he's only interested in one thing."

He doesn't and he is, I thought. Suddenly I felt very close to Dell's mom and dad. If they were here, high fives all around.

"Can you believe it?" she asked.

Mentally I took back the high fives. "Well," I said.

"You don't agree with them?" She looked horrified.

"Of course not," I lied. "Not exactly."

"You do. You do agree with them. You think Marshall just wants to get me into bed?"

Get me into bed. I've always had trouble with that expression. It's a little too not true for me. Along with "sleeping together." Please. "I think he wants to have sex with you," I said.

"Maybe that's what I want, too," she said. Her face went crimson.

"Oh."

"Oh?"

"I thought you wanted to wait."

"I have waited."

"I thought you meant *wait* wait, not wait for the weekend."

"We've been going out since the beginning of the year and before we broke up we were together for months. What am I waiting for? Maybe it's like Mr. Truelove says, I'm living an inauthentic life. Living in a wasteland."

"Hold on there," I said, with no idea where to go next. "Just hold your horses."

She stood there, holding her horses, but I had nothing.

"I'm tired of wait waiting," she said. "I feel like I've been wait waiting my whole life for something to happen."

"This isn't an 'unfortunate event' situation, is it?" Ever since Lemony Snicket's *A Series of Unfortunate Events*, Dell's been waiting for hers to start. She cried and cried when the orphans got the letter from their dead parents (a very fortunate bit of timing I thought, considering the title) and I said, whoa, girl, it's just a movie. She said that was the point, it *was* just a movie to her because she'd never had an unfortunate event, let alone a series of unfortunate events, but it was real to other people. People like me, she meant. Like I said, she's always romanticizing my tragedies. "Trust me," I said. "Unfortunate events are way, way, way overrated."

"Thanks for assuming that if I sleep with Marshall it will be an unfortunate event."

"Sleep?" I couldn't help myself.

"Be with, then."

"Be with? You want to *be* with him? Couldn't you *be* with him at a movie?"

"It's just an expression."

"No, it's not. I'm pretty sure it's an action. From what I've heard."

"Why do you care how I say it?"

"Because words are important to you and you can't even say it."

"I can so say it."

"Then say it."

"I don't have to say it."

I kept my big fat trap shut, but I was thinking, Yes, you do. I think you have to be able to say it and you have to hear yourself say it for it to be real.

Chapter Eleven

Dad had been pretty sporadic in the renovating department, showing up every day for a week and then not at all for a couple of weeks. (He said that a paying gig came up. I wondered when he started saying things like "paying gig.") He'd managed to tear down a chunk of the wall between Angela's room and mine and that was about it. The plan was to create a third room, taking some of my current space and some of Angela's space (my old space) and then slip a new wall in there like one of those shoebox projects I used to have to do in elementary school. My wall looked like something from a botched terrorist attack, ragged and dispirited. I hung an old plaid blanket that my great-aunt somebody made for me over it. Angela, I noticed, had hung her yoga mat.

"Nice to see you on the job, Workman," I said.

"Is that a dig?"

"Yes, indeed." I slumped my backpack on the bed. "Also, I wanted to tell you how much I'm enjoying the drywall dust — the way it's clogging my adolescent pores and giving me an elderly hacking cough."

"Work-in-progress, Funny Face," he said, but he was

mostly ignoring me as he wrestled with a stubborn piece of plaster.

Sometimes I wondered if he was dragging the project out because he wanted to spend more time with me, and sometimes I wondered if that was just wishful thinking. He used to be a History/Woodworking teacher, though. Obviously the man understands time and wood. That's all I'm saying.

But here was the weird part: my mother wasn't freaking out. My mother, who loved nothing more than to have everything in its place, was curiously okay with a gaping hole in one of her walls. What would Freud think? I figured it had something to do with Little Sir Whatsit and the fact that her doctor had warned her about high blood pressure, but even so, it was weird. It was weirder than that; it was zen.

In fact, there was far too much zen going on around here. Most days I'd come home and find wooden flute and sitar music wafting through the plaid blanket/yoga mat wall like the fumes of the lentil crap that boiled below in the kitchen and I'd think, What happened to my life? But everybody else seemed okay with it. Mom in her preggo yoga tights, Angela in her form-hugging Lululemons, Cal in his spandex. Okay, it didn't take a rocket scientist to see what was happening. There was too little blood circulation. Thanks to my loose pants, I was the only one getting enough oxygen to my brain.

"What's with the blanket?" Dad asked.

"It's holding up the house," I said.

He shook his head. "I meant the one over the mirror."

I looked at the shrouded chest of drawers in the corner. I'd almost forgotten about my "experiment." Even at school I automatically avoided my reflection in the bathroom mirrors. You might be surprised to know that you actually have to look if you want to see yourself. You have to focus. It was turning into a bit of a game and I was winning. I mean, how necessary was it to have a daily glimpse of one's self? How much will have changed? How brilliant does a person have to be to locate their lips or eyelashes for gloss and mascara? "It's a psychology experiment." I gave him my prepared explanation. "For school."

He stopped prying at the stubborn wall. "How is George doing, by the way?"

I considered giving him a rundown of today's bizarre behavior, but decided against it. Dell was too much a part of the whole thing and I was afraid if I started talking, I wouldn't stop. That was a pattern my dad and I had gotten into. He missed so much of the regular day-to-day stuff that, when I was with him, I tended to babble to fill in the blanks. There's the whole other approach, the pass-the-remote-control route, but I've opted for the babble-till-you-drop package. It makes him feel needed. Even so, today, babble would be risky. "Swell," I said.

"He's growing a ponytail."

"I wondered about that."

"It's not a good sign."

"A sign?" I said, despite my good intentions of minimal engagement.

"I'm a little worried about him."

"It's not that bad," I said. "It's probably just a phase. Like that goatee you used to have."

"That was handsome and manly." He wrestled with the wall. A chunk came off.

"Yes, indeed. Handsome."

He smiled at the wall. I couldn't see it, but I knew. I felt the old lurch of my heart at how great it was having him here — at the way, here, he still knew me. And then it lurched again at knowing that soon he would be gone again. Away from my everyday life. Parents should never leave first. It was as wrong as rain rising. You could come up with all the plausible explanations in the world and it still added up to wrong, wrong, wrong.

He pulled his work gloves off and sat on the edge of my bed. "I'm a little worried about him," he said again.

"Oh."

"He was served with his divorce papers over the weekend."

"Oh."

My dad interpreted my one-syllable response as interest. "Before Christmas. What timing." Here's something that might not be a well-known fact:

divorced parents assume that because they have gone through a seismic event, their children will be interested in sifting through the fallout.

"Rough," I said. Even a chimpanzee parent should be able to pick up on such minimal interest.

"No kidding," he said as though I'd offered a deep insight. "The holidays are the worst. He was still hoping for a reconciliation, for Pete's sake."

I tried a noncommittal "hmm," all the while rooting through my backpack. "Man, I can't believe all the homework I have to do over the holidays," I said.

"He's got two little kids," my dad continued, like I'd said nothing. "Jeremy and somebody else with a J ... Josephine, that's it."

"Josephine? For real?" I was sucked in despite myself.

"He named her after Jo March in *Little Women*. It was his favorite book as a kid."

"Ooo-kaaay."

Dad smiled. "Too much information?"

I shrugged.

"I'm just worried about him."

"You said, like three times."

"Ooo-kaaay," he said.

I smiled.

He put his work gloves on again. "So, your mother and I were talking." His voice was different now, business. "She's invited me for Christmas Eve. Would that be too weird?"

I was torn between *Yes* and *Duh.* "Mildly," I decided.

"Really?" He seemed surprised. That's the thing that baffles me the most about my parents. They've been on this planet for forty years and they still manage to look surprised at the most obvious things. Forty years! It would be like Moses saying, *Oh look, a cactus!* "Well, if that's how you feel, I don't have to come."

"Of course you do," I said quickly. "It would be great. Very ... blended."

He brightened. "That's what we thought."

There it was again — the "we" word. I coaxed a smile from my smarter self, who wanted to scream instead.

"So, you're okay with that?"

I said yes in a way that even a gerbil parent would have been able to see through, but not my dad. He looked pleased — happy even. But then I thought about how he wouldn't have to go to some diner on Christmas Eve, and that, at least, was a good thing.

As I watched him hack away at a wall that had really never done anything wrong except to stand where it was told, I thought that — as a family — we weren't blending so much as congealing.

Chapter Twelve

We used to open presents on Christmas Morning, but this year my mother decided that we should change the tradition. Christmas Eve, she decided, would be more magical.

The dinner was actually quite pleasant. My dad and Cal seemed to take the blurry twinkling lights and the falling snow outside as a personal challenge to be charming and delightful. It was almost as if they were trying to out-charm the other. My dad offered to bring the stuffing and arrived right on time with an armful of presents and wine and sparkling juice for my mom. Cal cooked the turkey and, when it was time to carve, he handed the blade over to my father. I had managed to sip at least a half a glass of my dad's wine, so I saw this as a scene out of a new and improved *Hamlet*. It was as if the new king (Claudius, I think) was saying, *You can kill me for marrying and impregnating your wife or you can take it out on a dead bird*. Maybe I had an entire glass, I'm not sure. All I know is that if Shakespeare had been a little more practical, a little more civilized, there might not have been a need for such messy revenge.

Dad sliced the turkey elegantly. We ate it with mashed potatoes (mine, with garlic), cranberry sauce (Angela's, with citrus zest), my father's stuffing (with fresh herbs) and my mother's store-bought pumpkin pie. She would have made one, she said, except she was pregnant. Nobody argued with her.

By the end of dinner I was completely looped. I'd never had anything to drink before, really, but it seemed like that kind of occasion. My dad and Cal weren't noticing because their charm had been bolstered by eggnog and wine, and my mother seemed too relieved that everyone was getting along to notice. Only Angela noticed.

She and I carried the empty plates into the kitchen. I was feeling pretty normal except for the fact that there seemed to be two partially demolished turkey carcasses on the countertop. "Didn't we just have one turkey?" I said.

Angela smiled. "Some of us did."

"Huh?"

"You're drunk."

"Noooo." Even I recognized the multiple use of the vowel "o" as a giveaway, especially the way it echoed inside my head. "Really? I only had, like, a sip."

"You've been *sipping* like a sailor all night. Your parents are clueless."

"My parents? What about your parents?" The plural was unfortunate for a couple of reasons: (a) the lingering "s" sounded drunk and (b) she only had one parent here. "Parent. What about *your* parent?" Then I felt a little sick so I sat down. "My parents are clueless."

Angela smiled. In my state, it seemed like the warmest, most genuine smile I'd seen from her. I wondered if maybe wine was a magic potion. Maybe it let people see through walls. People walls, I mean, not the kind with a blanket on one side and a yoga mat on the other. That was easy to see through because of the missing plaster. Maybe if people had holes in them we would all get along better? See, I wasn't drunk. This was brilliant stuff.

I rested my head on the countertop. I waited for the room to stop spinning and for more brilliance to shine down on me. I closed my eyes, but that made the spinning worse. My stomach was churning like a high-powered washing machine. I quickly opened my eyes to see if this would help. Angela was behind the counter, wearing an apron and loading the dishwasher.

"Do you want a cup of coffee or do you need to throw up?" she asked.

"You sound like the world's worst waitress."

Angela laughed. Now her laughter sounded more real than usual. What was happening to me? I was a sage or something.

"You know," I said carefully, "coffee would probably be a nice drink right now. I would appreciate a cup of coffee."

Angela poured a cup and put it in front of me. "Here's a tip. When you're drunk, use as few words as possible. Drunk people talk too much. They're too self-conscious. They think everyone is looking at them because, well, everyone is. But if drawing attention to yourself is not your goal, try to ease into the woodwork."

"Like, be a wall?"

Angela laughed again. "Do you want milk?"

"I am drinking coffee."

"I meant in your coffee. And don't forget your contractions. Drunk people always forget their contractions."

I nodded wisely, trying to remember what a contraction was. "Oh, no. What are they? I do forget them."

It sounded like she was giggling. "No, you don't. See, there's one. Don't. Do not."

"Don't what?" I sounded a little hysterical.

Angela was definitely giggling now. She leaned her head against the cupboard; her cheeks were pink, tears streaming down her face.

Suddenly they all came back to me: shouldn't, can't, don't. "Okay, I get it."

But she was still laughing. I'd never seen her like this before. She was different, a different version. Truer.

"You are, I mean, you're very pretty, did you know?"

She took a paper towel and blew her nose. "So they tell me."

"But you are, really. I mean, if I looked like you, I would stand in front of the mirror all day long. I would actually get nothing done in my life."

"You're pretty, too." She smiled, but her face wasn't as real as it was before. "Drink your coffee."

"I'm cute," I said. "I mean, I like the way I look," I tried to remember. It had been sort of a long time. I picked up a spoon and took a peek. It surprised me that I was upside down, but not overly.

Angela turned the spoon around so I popped right side up again.

"Wow," I said. But I was so blurry I had to look closer to make out my features. Either it was a defective spoon or I had a really long face.

Angela put the last dish into the machine.

"But you're beautiful," I continued. "How does that work?"

"Drink up," she said.

"No, really. How does it feel? I want to know."

She shrugged. "Beauty is in the eye of the beholder."

"Phhhht."

"No, really." She wasn't smiling anymore. "Something is only beautiful if somebody says it is. The beholder part. It just makes you beholden. Obligated."

"To be pretty?"

"Sort of."

"Like it's your job?" Obviously I needed another sip of wine, just a sip, for this to make sense.

Angela wiped a drop of coffee off the countertop. Then she took my cup, wiped the drips and returned it to me. "No, not like a job. It's ... weird. Never mind."

"No, really, this is fascinating." I stumbled over the word, had to say it twice.

"You aren't even going to remember this conversation tomorrow."

"I so will," I said indignantly, pronouncing each word carefully. I took another sip of coffee. "So if it's not a job ...?"

"Listen, I'm not saying it's not great, okay? I'm not complaining. I'm just saying."

"You're not really, actually saying, er, much."

She put both hands flat on the counter. "People look at me, a lot. They like what they see and so that's who I have to be."

"Have to?"

"Well, whatever. It's easier, okay? It's better. I can just be her."

"Her? What about you?" It was starting to come together.

She started wiping the counter again. Her fingerprints, I guessed, since that was all that was left. She was really thorough.

"That doesn't matter. They just want to see the shell, the container, the ... mask."

"The version?"

She sighed. "I guess."

"But what about you? Who sees you?"

"Seriously? Who would want to? Trust me on that one."

I had nothing to say to this.

She laughed and the sound was brittle. "If you do remember this little talk tomorrow, I'll deny it."

And then my mother came in. Even through my hazy state, I could see that she was taking in the scene.

"You're drinking coffee?" she asked suspiciously.

I remembered Angela's advice. "Yes, I'm."

I followed my mother and Angela into the living room. By the time we sat down, Angela had her party face on. She smiled, tossed her hair and giggled at something my dad said. When she looked over at me I couldn't even see a glimpse of Kitchen Angela. The Version had returned. Except that it looked sad, and then, just like that, she looked away. Time to sneak another sip.

"Jes?"

I jumped. "Yes?"

"Do you want to be Santa?"

It was my mother's new, blended voice, but an old question. She'd forgotten the new us, forgotten the two new people. They wouldn't understand that it was okay to be corny and cheesy on Christmas Eve and pretend that Santa really existed ... that it was a game that we played between the four of us — the other four of us. I had a headache; I needed another sip.

"I am ... I'm ... an elf," I said.

"Okay. Angela, how about you?" My mother was undaunted. "Do you want to hand out the gifts?"

"Sure," Angela said.

As I opened my presents, I realized it took a bit of work to appear sober, but I think I did a good job. When I got the regular things from my dad — books, journals, perfume — I amazed myself by how happy and genuine I could seem. It was like watching a little movie of me: *This Is How I Act.* That would be the title. Cal gave me a book as well, *A Room of One's Own*, apologizing that it was the same book that my dad gave me. That could have been awkward. But, thank you, wine, no awkward moment for me. I was too busy trying to be normal. It's probably self-absorbed of me that I can't recall who got what, but I was really preoccupied with all the colors and glints of silver and gold in the ribbons and the way they caught the lights of the Christmas tree in a way that's fairly amazing if you squint. I sipped now and again. I don't think anyone really noticed. It occurred to me that maybe nobody wanted to notice, but I shoved the thought away because it wasn't very Christmassy.

After everything that could be exchanged had been exchanged and we'd all oohed and aahed, I followed Angela's lead cleaning up the sparkling debris. I felt a little sad that all the beautiful packages had been dismembered. Bad attitude, I told myself, taking another sip of something in my father's glass that was now brownish. Had the wine turned brown? Did wine do that?

"Eww," I said, without thinking.

My dad looked at me curiously, a why-are-you-doing-that look, but said nothing. As his concern melted into denial before my all-seeing eyes, I suddenly recognized how a person really could get away with a lot when guilt was in charge. Guilt: the worst babysitter ever. Another brilliant thought.

"We're not quite done," my mother chirped suddenly. "Sit down, Angela."

Then she and Cal disappeared mysteriously into the hallway. For an awkward moment the three of us sat at our places. My dad took another slug of the swamp drink.

"Thanks again for the book, Steven," Angela said politely.

But there was more than politeness in her voice. It was plain as day, as plain as the pert nose on her flawless face. She was flirting with my father. Oh sure, this would be impossible to prove in a court of law, but it was true. It wasn't her words — they were proper enough — it was the way she shifted her perfect proportions in his direction, not to mention the luxurious blond hair flip.

Suddenly my father's glass was irresistible to me — or, rather, the murky fluid therein. Especially since he was falling for Angela's wily ways. He ... did he just blush? Was he ... discomfited? At the shifting of her perfect properties, er, proportions?

I was about to bellow, *She will not be my new stepmother. She will not*, when Mom and Cal came back into the room.

They were carrying boxes — plain, unadorned except for perforations along the lids. I immediately thought of air and how I needed some. I got up to open a window, but my mother said, "Sit down." Her tone wasn't quite so blended anymore and the words came out gruffly.

"When did sitting become so all-fired important to you?" I barked back. (And wondered when I started saying "all-fired.")

She paused. My mother has a very hard time passing up a question. "Just sit," she said.

She placed her box in front of Angela. Cal placed his in front of me. I wondered if they'd had a dress rehearsal for this clearly symbolic moment.

And then the lid on my box shifted. This seemed very portentous to me, and I sat back, alarmed.

Angela dove into the moment and the box. And then she was holding a kitten — white, longhaired, green-eyed, beautiful, snotty-looking even though so young. "Oh," she said. "She's perfect."

In that moment, I recognized my mother's true gift: playing to the patently obvious. And I knew what must come next.

Awkwardly, I lifted the lid to my box. There, huddled in the corner, of an indiscriminate color and small, was a puppy. It was ... the ugliest puppy I'd ever seen. "Murff," it snorted up at me.

"Well?" said my mother.

I scooped it up gingerly and held it at arm's length to get a better look. The alcohol in my bloodstream had not deceived me. It was an ugly puppy. "Well, look at you," I said because I obviously had to say something.

"He's a mutt," Cal said, catching my eye.

"A crossbreed," my mother said. I felt her scowl. I felt her expectation. The pressure in the room was as real as the empty cardboard box or the couch I was sitting on.

"It's a he?" I said.

"I think so," said Cal. "He's a rescue."

Don't you just love symbolism?

Chapter Thirteen

"She gets the longhaired purebred," I said. "I get the ugly mutt."

Dell held the puppy up to her nose. "Who's the little baby puppy-wuppy? Who's the wittle, dittle puppy-wuppy? Who's not ugly-wugly?"

"Oh, my," I said, taking him from her.

"Stay for brunch," she said as I headed for the door. "My mom's making blintzes. With cottage cheese." She scowled, I think so that I would know this was supposed to be a bad thing.

"Can't. I just wanted to show you the newest misfit."

"I would come with you, but Pammy's here and ..."

"I know." Evil Pammy had returned from college for Christmas break. Dell had grumbled over having to listen to a sister who never stopped talking about herself and whose biggest woe was gaining the Freshman Five pounds. (Pammy would never, ever gain the Freshman Fifteen.)

Earlier, I had given Dell my traditional gift: a leather-bound journal full of empty pages. She gave me a super-über-feminine bustier that any Bond girl would have been proud of: lace, shiny stuff, gauze — an ejection button, probably. I held it up in front of me, turned it around, thinking it might make more sense that way. "Thanks. This is quite something," I said. I was a little surprised that I hadn't received the usual "books that Dell loved." Last year it was *Madame Bovary*. I was about halfway through before I realized that this gal was traveling fast down the short road to nowhere good.

"Quite what?" she asked.

"Flimsy?"

"It will accent your décolletage."

On an already sad morning — hungover, a Christmas Day first — nothing seemed sadder than Dell using an Angela word. But Dell had apparently forgotten its origin, sadder still.

She walked to the end of the sidewalk with me.

"He cried all night long," I said as the puppy squiggled in my arms.

"He misses his mommy," she said, nose to wet nose. "Don't you, little Mr. Puppy-Wupperson?"

"Stop," I ordered, but I had to laugh.

"Merry Christmas," she said, giving me one more hug. "Enjoy your lingerie." Then she winked, and this undid me. True, I wasn't tightly wrapped, but still.

"Oh, that's what it is! I really don't ... Maybe you should keep it?" I didn't mean this in a harsh way, but honestly.

"You don't like it?" Now she looked like *she* was going to come undone.

"No, I do. I love it. It's beautiful." I was sorry that I'd said anything, but mostly I was sorry that I'd said it when my head was beating like a steel band.

"You don't."

"I do. It's just that I think I'm asexual."

Tears that had begun to brim on her lower lids seemed to be sucked up by some magnetic force. "What?"

"I read an article on it," I said. "Apparently there's this rising movement of teenagers who feel that sex is not for them."

"Well, who's it for then?"

Not a bad question. But now was not the time to be sidetracked. "Seriously, in this day and age, sex is so out there, so prevalent, that people — teens — think they're freaks if they don't want it. But not everybody is built the same way, Dell. Not everybody wants to have sex."

"In this day and age?"

"That's right. Everybody jumping into bed with each other ... willy nilly."

"Willy nilly?"

I ignored the smirk on her face. She crossed her arms ... maybe to keep warm, but probably to look smug. "So you don't think about what it would be like to kiss Sam?"

Curses, hell and Moses in the Desert. Why had I ever told her about that? "No. I don't. Gotta go."

I heard her calling after me. "Your puppy needs a name."

"Merry X," I called back.

• • •

I looked at his house as I walked past. Thought about going inside. It would be great. There would be Christmas chaos and mayhem and yelling and craziness. Shouting and tears and laughter. And Sam, being cute, taking pictures. They would welcome me and feed me and not ask questions. Well, Danny would ask questions, but then Henry would thump him and Amber would plead for sanity to reign, etc., etc. I'd be spared having to answer why I wasn't home on Christmas morning.

The truth was I was hungover and Mom and Cal and Angela were still sleeping; we'd done everything Christmassy last night. I was supposed to go to my dad's on Christmas Day because that's what the court order said. That's what court orders do. Nobody ever asks the kid how gross it is that a total stranger gets to decide where you spend Christmas. Nobody thinks about how sick it is that their parents are in such a humiliating place that they can't decide who should have the kid for Christmas.

"Muuuh," said puppy. I assumed this was baby dog for *arf*.

"You really do need a name," I said. I held the squiggling mass of warmth next to me because it was pretty freaking cold out here.

As I stood for a while, looking at the house of great happiness, my stomach twisted with loneliness and I knew I wouldn't go inside. They were the zany troubadours of love and I couldn't handle that right now.

My head banged like a loose shutter as I walked through streets that were mostly empty. The city was great in the summer when the tourists came, but a little sad when it was being ignored. The wind blew snow from curb to curb like a game of air hockey with no puck.

When I reached the corner, the first thing I saw was the spire of a church against the washed-out sky. I used to want to go inside when I was a kid because I thought it was neat to have something spiky pointing out of the roof. But my parents were torn about how to raise me — Godwise — so we'd only done religion a few times. (My dad was disillusioned and my mother was confused. I remember a Buddhist temple and a Sikh temple and somebody's basement where everybody's hands were in the air.) We went to a regular church a couple of times, but not since my baby sister's funeral. But it wasn't this church. This one was old-fashioned, quaint — kind of fairy-tale. It was that spire, reaching up, spindly and bold, daring a lightning bolt to hit it.

It occurred to me then that a church might be a very Christmas-morning place to be. I wasn't sure where they stood on hangovers and puppies, but I thought I'd give it a shot.

When I walked through the doors, I heard music. I wasn't such a heathen that I didn't recognize "Silent Night." It was nice. I also remembered the story of Moses. For some reason, Moses had been featured on the flannel-board all three times I had been to Sunday school. The story had lingered—probably because his parents had sent him floating down the river in a basket. That never seemed very responsible to me.

I found a seat in the back. People around me smiled. I wondered what they got for Christmas. I wondered if they were hungover. They didn't look like it, but maybe I didn't either. Mostly I tried to look inconspicuous because, well, I was with puppy.

After the songs, the head guy started to talk about Jesus, naturally, but my mind kept going back to that story of Moses. The dude did not have an easy life, except for a few brief years in the Pharoah's palace ... although I may be mixing my facts up with *The Emperor's New Groove*, and I'm not sure how historical that was. But between being dumped and sent down the river in a basket, killing a man a few years later, getting a talking-to by God from a burning bush (that had to be a highlight, I think) and finally being forced to be the leader of his people even though he specifically turned down the job, old Moses had a pretty action-packed life. And, at the end of it, after heroically trudging through the desert for forty years with a bunch of grumbling relatives, he doesn't even get to enter the land of milk and honey. And why? I forget. I think it had something to do with making a mistake along the way that really pissed God off. Nice. One mistake. He had to be thinking, What was the point? So much for the hero's trudge.

"Murff," said the lump beneath my coat. A woman in a pair of jeans and a shimmery top that Angela would kill for glanced over. I smiled at her. "Merry Christmas," I said.

She nodded politely. I tried to listen. We were at the part where Herod ordered all the babies murdered because he'd heard that a future king had been born. He was thorough, I guess. Merry Christmas, my big butt. Man, what a brutal world. But the guy hurried on to say that Jesus arrived in Egypt safely — ironic, I thought, considering everything Moses did to get his people out of Egypt — and eventually he grew up to save the world. The world. I let the words sink in. Save the world? The whole entire world?

The room was silent; everyone was taking in this monumental, if slightly unlikely, news. Too quiet, apparently, for young puppy, who whimpered loudly. This time people from surrounding pews turned to look at me, not just Shimmery Top beside me.

"Are you all right, dear?" asked a very wrinkly but kind-eyed old lady.

"Too much turkey," I whispered. Lame, I know, but it suddenly seemed wrong to have a dog in church. More wrong than telling a lie in church? Probably not, but the words just slipped out. Unfortunately, so did puppy's head, right between the second and third button. He looked relieved to be breathing fresh air. His chubby tongue popped out of his squashed, furry little face and he panted at the air.

"Oh, dear," said the lady, whose face, I have to say, bore some resemblance to his.

"I should go," I whispered, grateful that I was sitting on the aisle and that the choir was assembling at the front, making at least a bit of noise.

"You should stay for Christmas cookies."

"Thanks, but I have to get going."

"God bless you."

"Okay, well, I appreciate that." I fled as the choir belted out "Joy to the World."

• • •

Outside, I placed the little troublemaker down on the snowy sidewalk. He looked up at me, shivering. "You should pee or something," I said.

He trundled over to a small snowbank that sparkled

in the sun like it had been sprayed with cut glass and left a slim yellow line in the snow. I picked him up again. "I've always wanted to do that," I said, putting his velvety snout close to mine. He was shaking quite vigorously so I tucked him back inside my coat.

"Let's get going, Moses." The name slipped out. But he licked me on the face like it was official.

On the way to my dad's apartment, I explained to Moses where things stood in the family department. I went into a fair bit of detail, causing a couple of Christmas Day dog walkers to look at me like maybe I shouldn't be out on my own. But then they'd see Moses and smile understandingly. It made me feel good that people didn't view talking to a dog as abnormal behavior, because the truth was I was starting to warm up to old Moses. It wasn't his fault that he was the ugliest puppy in the world.

But looks weren't everything. If anyone knew that it was me. I hadn't seen my reflection in three months and I was still here, wasn't I? Existing like crazy. Okay, bad choice of words. The whole thing was starting to feel a little crazy, even to me.

"So, in conclusion, Moses, last night's parents are the current Mom and Dad and now we're going to visit your human-father once removed. It's still a little unclear how that happened, but apparently these things gain greater clarity with time and we can expect to grow hugely because of it." He looked up at me with his melted semi-sweet chocolate eyes. I waited for him to blink; I couldn't believe how long it took. He was looking at me like I was the most important thing in his entire life, like he couldn't tear his eyes away. Lassie could be on TV and he still wouldn't look away. How could that be? We had just barely met. I was still waiting for him to blink when I bumped into a telephone pole.

"Aieee. That really hurt." For some reason he looked devastated by the tone in my voice. (Due to pain.) "But it's not your fault." He blinked. "Now you blink. Thanks for that. Well, here we are. I hope he has dog food." Moses squiggled in my arms. "Oh, crap. That's Mr. Truelove. He's my teacher at school. What is he doing here on Christmas Day? Oh, Holy Moses in the Desert." I glanced down quickly. "No offense."

Moses looked at me as though no offense had been taken, as though there was nothing in the world I could ever do that could offend him. Why didn't everyone have a dog? I could not believe the adoration in his eyes. But first things first. How to avoid Mr. Truelove? I was barely coping with my own sad family; I could not handle a surrogate sad-family situation. Ugh.

I did the only thing a reasonable person could do under the circumstances. I hid. I hid behind the snarly fronds of a bush. "What now?" I asked.

Moses looked up at me as if to say, *I'm a puppy. What do I know?* And then he barked like an actual dog for the first time. Of course I would get a dog with bad timing. It figured.

I ducked down quickly. Mr. Truelove was looking our way — what if he thought the bush was talking to him? I did not want to be responsible for that. I peeked through the shrubbery, hunkered down, until he entered the building.

I waited until the door was closed and I was sure that the elevator would have hauled Mr. Truelove up to his apartment. I tried not to think about the paper bag under his arm and what it might contain — booze, dirty magazines, razor blades? Instead I imagined a nice turkey club sandwich and a couple of heart-warming movies. That's what Dell would believe. So I went with that.

• • •

"*La visa nave da?*" I guessed at the Spanish version of Merry Christmas into the speaker. Dad buzzed me in with a garbled version of "Hark, I'll Let My Daughter In."

In the hallway, I decided that somebody was definitely having turkey curry. Moses's nose was going at maximum sniffing speed. When I walked into the apartment, the smell became stronger. "Whoa," I got out before I started to cough. "Christmas around the world?"

"I think it's going to be very good, although the turmeric cap did fall into the sauce so it's a little more fluorescent than I would like. He gave me a big hug. "Merry Christmas, Pumpkin Soup."

"Same to you, Squash Racquet."

"*Feliz Navidad*," came a voice from the living room.

"Jes, guess who dropped by?"

I turned to see Mr. Truelove taking off his coat — not a good sign. "Well, hey," I said. "Hey there."

"Don't you mean, 'ho, ho'?" Dad smiled awkwardly.

"Yeah, that's exactly what I meant," I said, turning my back to Mr. Truelove — all the better to give my dad a what-were-you-thinking stare.

"*Feliz Navidad*," he said again, with precision. "I think that's what you were trying to say."

"Good to know."

"Little boys' room?"

My dad pointed down the teeny-tiny hallway to the only room that could possibly be the washroom. Mr. Truelove giggled. "Of course, same as my apartment."

Dad and I smiled as though he'd told a joke until the door was closed. The smile fell off both our faces at the same time.

"I'm sorry. He just dropped by with a Christmas gift." He pointed to a six-pack of beer on the table, like this scene couldn't get any more pathetic. "What could I say?"

"Er, maybe that you were having dinner with your daughter ... and a friend." I put Moses down on the floor.

"Oh, you brought the ugliest puppy in the world. Where did your mother find him?"

"He's not ugly," I said, suddenly believing this with all my heart. "He's ..." I struggled to find a way to describe the scrunched-in face and mottled fur and the way his tongue didn't quite seem to fit inside his mouth, making him look not too bright. "Don't change the subject."

"I'm sorry."

A muffled crash came from the direction of the bathroom, followed closely by another giggle. "Oops."

"That towel rack is loose. Don't worry about it," Dad called.

"Is he okay?"

Before he could answer, Mr. Truelove was back and pulling a beer loose from the plastic ring. As he passed me, he smiled and said, "Nice to see you. You look good." He gave Moses a little pat on the head then pulled the tab off the beer and took a sip. He walked into the living room and turned on the television.

"Thanks," I said, not sure if he was talking to me or to the puppy. To my father, I mouthed, *Is he drunk?*

"A little," he whispered.

"On Christmas Day?"

Dad's eyebrows went up. "Because Christmas Eve is so much better?"

Oops. "I'll just go entertain our guest."

"Good idea."

"Hey," Mr. Truelove said as I sat down on the chair in the corner. "I hope it's not too strange, me being here? Your dad said he had lots of food, so ..."

"It's great." I shook my head. "I'm spending New Year's with Ms. Blanchard."

Mr. Truelove gave me a blank stare.

"The principal?" I hate having to explain a joke.

He nodded as though I was serious. I looked helplessly at my dad, who — hard to believe — was smirking. "Ohhh," Mr. Truelove said. "That's funny. You're funny, you know that? And a good student." He tapped the side of his head. "Always thinking. I told your dad you're going places."

"Well, I am."

He waited.

I got off the chair. "I'm going to help my dad with the rice."

He chuckled right away at this one, no doubt warming up to the idea that today was going to be one big laugh riot. I had barely crossed the tiny little border into the relative safety of the kitchen when he gave up a great howl. My dad and I both jumped and rushed back into the room.

Mr. Truelove was on his feet, holding Moses at

arm's length. The front of his shirt was soaking wet. For a minute I was afraid he was going to hurl the puppy across the room, but instead he just looked into Moses's eyes and said solemnly, "That's okay, little guy. I'm used to it."

I rushed over and grabbed Moses. "I'm so sorry. He's just ... new." Mr. Truelove flapped at his chest as though this would somehow dry him off. I ran to the bathroom, got a towel and handed it to him. He dabbed at his shirt in little staccato bursts.

My dad spread some newspapers on the kitchen floor. "Bring him over here."

"Who?" I asked. I was starting to enjoy this. And pretty sure that this degree of humiliation would sway the grading curve in my direction.

Dad took Moses and placed him down on the floor.

"Current events are going to help, how?"

"It's how you house-train him."

"And you're so experienced."

"I potty-trained you, didn't I?"

I looked over at Mr. Truelove to see if he'd heard. He was still dabbing, but also smiling. I shrugged. "Yes, they used newspapers for me also. It was quite experimental."

Mr. Truelove pointed a finger at me as he sat back down on the couch with the towel spread over his chest like a bib. "Funny. You're funny."

• • •

That was the tone of the entire day. We played Scrabble and Monopoly and, finally, poker. Mr. Truelove showed no sign of leaving. Ever. In between beers, my dad slipped glasses of cranberry juice over to Mr. Truelove and encouraged him to eat the turkey curry that was as yellow as, well, his shirt. (My dad offered him a fresh one; he refused.) As the light grew dim, I noticed that Dad had thrown some Christmas lights over the bookcase and, while there was no tree, he'd decked out his fig plant quite nicely; there were even a few ornaments weighing down the delicate branches. All through dinner and then through pumpkin pie, we listened to Mr. Truelove try to recite the lines to *A Christmas Carol* along with the TV. He really got into it, especially the Ghost of Christmas Past. It had to be the most ridiculous Christmas ever — but not the saddest. That would have been the Christmas after Alberta died, or maybe the one when my parents were separated and everyone was pretending that it wasn't sad. So, I'll take ridiculous.

Shortly after Tiny Tim proclaimed, "God bless us, everyone," Mr. Truelove staggered to his feet. There's no point sugarcoating it — he was staggering. For one horrifying moment, at the door, I thought he was going to hug me good-bye, but he just leaned forward and nodded. "Really. God bless us, everyone." Then he waved to Moses and, after promising my dad that he was going straight to his apartment, he was gone.

Dad leaned against the door and pressed it shut with his back. "I owe you one, kiddo."

I held up my hands and spread my fingers apart. "You owe me ten."

He smiled and nodded. "Let's leave the dishes and watch the fig tree for a while, okay?" He looked tired.

"Backgammon?"

"I'd hate to kick your ass on Christmas Day."

"Such a hopeful man you are," I said, happy to return to sitcom mode. As I went into the bedroom to look for the game, I heard a knock at the door. "He forgot his coat," I said, seeing it on the bed.

When I came back, my dad had a little red-haired person wrapped around his middle. And there was another one, larger, also redheaded, waiting in line. The tallest of the crimson trio was closing the door behind her. My lightning-quick intellect figured out that she was the mom. "Is this her?" she said, smiling brightly at me. "You must be Jes. I'm Billi," she said, like I must know this already.

"Ho, ho," I said, waving the backgammon game at them.

"Ho, ho, ho," said the littlest one, releasing my father. "That's what Santa says."

"Um, Jes, this is Billi," said Dad. He pointed to the little girl who was staring up at me with such intensity that I thought I must have dinner in my teeth. "That's Holly."

"Like in Christmas," she yelled.

"Whoa, I'm right here." I smiled.

"And this is Marmalade." He put his hand on the taller one's shoulder.

"Excuse me?"

"Like the jam?" she said, rolling her eyes.

The mom — the Billi — smiled at me. "It changes. Last week it was Melody." She had that eager look on her face like she was about to *get to know me*.

I smiled back and quickly moved into the kitchen to start the dishes.

The two girls sauntered into the living room in a manner that could only be called familiar. Then they spied Moses and rushed over to him.

Holly screamed, "I love you!"

Marmalade said, "What's wrong with his face?"

"Sorry about this, Steven," Billi said. "I just wanted to stop by with some Christmas baking."

"That's great," Dad said, taking a platter of cookies from her.

I took a closer look at this woman who was gazing at my father with adoration spewing from her very pores. She was probably in her early thirties, slender but athletic-looking, curly auburn hair. Her skin was pale, dusted across her nose with freckles. What kind of grown-up has freckles, I thought. Dell would call her skin luminous. Stupid Dell.

"What's his name?" Holly screamed.

"Moses," I said.

"That's a dumb name," said Jam Girl.

I didn't say anything. I couldn't. I suddenly saw between the two of them, between their ages, my sister. All the ages that she'd never be or would have been. That's a tense, isn't it — would have been? She would have been. Third-person singular, future perfect. What the future would have been if she hadn't died. I wonder if that's all you got, one shot at the future perfect. I looked over at my dad and I knew that he was reading my face.

"I don't want to interrupt," Billi said.

"No, it's okay. I was just leaving." I had to get out of here before I did something stupid like cry.

"No, Jes. Don't go."

"I should ... get back." I grabbed my coat off the chair and headed to the door.

"I'll drive you."

"I should walk. Moses needs the exercise and it's nice out — all cool and crisp and even." I tried to think of something else to say because I was almost out the door, almost safe. "Good old King Wenceslas. Thanks for the Feast of Stephen." But he followed me out into the hallway. I kept walking toward the elevator. "It's not late. I'll be fine."

I pushed the button and hoped for a Christmas miracle that would make the world's slowest elevator defy its nature. Then I made a mistake and looked at my dad's face, the broken face that he usually hides. He hugged me. I buried my face in his chest and I whispered that lie I've always hated: "It'll be okay."

• • •

The streetlights sparkled on a skiff of snow and the air was still. The few people out were either drugged with turkey hormones or content to let the day move past the mayhem. It had almost been a merry Christmas, I thought. I tucked Moses deep inside my coat.

Grief has a way of hiding around a corner. You think it's gone, but when you finally have the courage to go around that corner, there it is waiting for you, smoking a cigarette, laughing at your foolishness. Grief is not kind.

Chapter Fourteen

"Tell me again about the part where Moses pees on Mr. Truelove."

I wrapped the blanket around my shoulders. We were sitting outside in my backyard — Sam, Dell and me. Sam, I had noticed, was almost Samlike when Dell was around. I was grateful for that. Better that than awkward failed-date Sam.

"Okay," I said. "Once more and then it's bedtime, Missy."

Dell smiled. Moses was curled up in her arms; he looked contented and moronic with his little tongue hanging out the side. Dell petted him constantly. She was a good aunt.

"So we hear this bellow, right? Like a raging moose, it was. I rushed in just in time to see Moses lifting his leg ... Mr. Truelove cowering in the corner, begging for mercy. Moses says, I swear, 'I've got you now.' Only in Spanish."

"Ohhh," said Dell, enjoying this new version. "Of course. He's bilingual."

"And then the pee was spraying every which way but north ... all over his shirt and pants and hair and ..."

"Not the hair. Not the thinning hair. Okay, that's too sad." She looked down at Moses. "She's lying, isn't she? You would never do such a thing."

I just shrugged. I had to tell them something, especially since I'd left out the drunken and disorderly part, not to mention Mr. Truelove saying that he was used to being peed on. Some things were just too pitiful to repeat. And I didn't want to tell them about the redheads.

"Well, your Christmas sounds much more interesting than mine. I had to stay awake all through Pammy: The College Years. Did you know that she's getting straight A's and has been asked out over a dozen times? Once, by a professor?"

"That could explain the A's," I said.

Dell smiled grimly. "And that they still do panty raids and her underwear is the most popular?"

"You could tell that story again," said Sam, smiling.

"What is it with guys and panties?" Dell scowled.

"I'm not overly fond of panties," he said, blushing.

I felt a pang of something like regret. Only it wasn't. Sam and I had made the best decision ever and I almost had my friend back.

"Dell," my mom called out the window. "Your mom wants you home. She's making a fondue."

"Okay," she smiled at my mom, but it immediately disappeared. "That would be fatty food dipped in batter and then submerged in fatty fat. Who puts batter in a fondue? She totally wants me to get fat."

She picked a chip out of the bag, looked at it and then dropped it again, as if remembering.

"Did you want me to cut that in half?" I said.

"I gained two pounds, I'll have you know."

"I'm going to call Weight Watchers. It's not too late. The first step is admitting you need help."

"So when's your next AA meeting?"

"Ooh." I was sorry that I'd ever told her about my Christmas Eve indiscretion. "Nicely played."

She handed Moses to me with a final kiss on his bumpy head. "You have to come to the New Year's party, okay? You, too, Sam. It'll be fun."

"I'll think about it," I said.

"Really think about it or pretend to think about it?"

"How does a person pretend to think? And, come to think of it, how would you know? Or am I pretending to think?"

"You are such a ... a ... an avoider."

"Nice word."

"Make her come, okay, Sam? It will be fun. Music and food and ..."

"And such?" I said.

Dell blushed. "I'll call you later."

"What's 'and such'?" Sam asked, once she'd left.

"Like et al," I improvised.

"Okay."

Suddenly the air was chillier; an iceberg had floated in between us. Just the tip, but you know what they say about icebergs.

"I should get going, too."

"Thanks for coming over. And thanks for my lamp."

"Yeah, well. Thanks for my food."

Now it was my turn to blush. "Well, you always need food, right?"

Once he left, I revisited the moment where I thought that food would be a good Christmas present. It's not like it was a last-minute decision. I'd agonized over it. I thought of giving him a T-shirt, but didn't that say, "I'd really like to see you in that shirt. Or, better yet, out of it"? Gloves were even worse because I'd probably blurt out something about his hands and the next thing you know we'd be talking about touching. Belt? Please. Food was safe, food was practical, food was a really good gift.

And what about a lamp? That was a little weird, wasn't it? When he gave it to me, I said, "Oh, you gave me a lamp."

He said, "I gave you a lamp."

"A lamp," I said.

"A lamp. You don't have to keep it."

I said that of course I wanted to keep it, who didn't need a lamp, and then I gave him his food. The whole thing was weird.

Dell, of course, thought it was extremely significant. "Maybe he's saying that you're the light of his life?" I had groaned. That was the first time I told her the Moses peeing story. There were worse things than being an avoider.

• • •

Angela was stretched out on the couch reading a book when I came in. *What's Up with Buddha?*

"Good book?" I put Moses down and he swaggled over to her. He tried to sit, but didn't quite have that mastered yet and toppled over. His legs flailed as he tried to right himself. Poor little chubby Moses. "No more fondue for you," I said, picking him up again.

Angela's kitten — Mariska or Marishma or Mahatma — looked disdainfully at him from her perch behind Angela's neck. Moses started barking, and no wonder — she was totally baiting him. Little Persian neck warmer. "Maybe he needs to go out," Angela said absently.

"He was just out."

Moses jumped off my lap, displaying great athletic promise, I thought. He stood with his legs splayed (it gave him more support) and resumed barking. The kitten slowly rose and then balanced (show-off) on the back of the couch; she arched her back, looking at him the whole time. Mocking, really. Moses went nuts, barking so hard that his chubby little self was practically levitating.

"He probably needs to go out," Angela repeated. "That's what they do when they're being trained. He's trying to communicate with you."

I had such a good comeback for Miss Serene and her great animal wisdom. The words were on their way when Moses suddenly stopped barking and pooped on the carpet. "Oh, crap," I said instead.

"That's right," Angela said, resuming her reading.

I almost had the stain removed when the doorbell rang. I looked at Angela, who made no move to get up. I swear the cat smirked. "I'll get that," I said. As I walked to the door, I called up the stairs. "Don't worry, I've got it." I did not need my ungainly mother walking into the room and seeing a not-quite-removed stain. She had already repeatedly asked what she had been smoking when she decided to get a dog. Never a second thought about that kitten, though.

The bell rang again. "Okay, okay, I'm coming." I opened the door.

My first thought was that I had never seen such a beautiful woman. Then I remembered that I had, almost.

"Angela, I think it's for you."

Chapter Fifteen

Her name was Bernadette. Angela whispered, later, that it was really Bernice, but she'd changed it. I almost died of joy when I heard that. I really don't know why.

And my mom's face when she saw her? One of those Kodak moments. I was actually pretty proud that I'd had the forethought to race upstairs and warn her, nice daughter that I am. Good thing. She was wearing her most comfortable pants, the ones with the big panel in the waist that none of the celebrities wear anymore, according to Angela, and a T-shirt that had BABY written on it with an arrow pointing down. I told her that we had a guest and who it was, and then I told her that she might want to reconsider her clothing.

My mom harrumphed at me and said that wouldn't be necessary. Then she caught a glimpse of Bernadette through the upstairs banister and did a one-eighty. I was holding her cute maternity outfit (Angela had picked it out for her at Trendy Mommies) when she returned.

"Thanks," she said, grabbing the outfit. "How ... how? How?"

"Deep breaths," I said, glad I'd been doing at least a little bit of baby labor research. "In and out, in and out. Sky of blue, fields of green."

"You're enjoying this?"

"Nooo," I said. "Not me. Maybe a little."

"How is it possible that she looks younger than Angela?"

"You only saw her from a distance."

"So she doesn't look good up close? She's actually hideous?" she asked hopefully.

"No. She's freakishly young-looking."

"But how?" She took off her clothes. I looked away. After she pulled on her cute outfit, she considered the mirror. She looked down at her makeup and then up at her face, as though the two were completely unrelated.

"Blush, I think, Mom. Maybe some lipstick."

"This is silly," she finally said as she applied eye shadow. "We're all grown-ups here. We are past this. And Cal loves me. He loves me the way I am." She pointed to her burgeoning stomach. "Hello? I didn't do this by myself. We have a connection, Jes. A real connection. I am a confident, mature, beautiful woman. And I'm real. This is real."

Was there anything more fun than watching my mother give herself therapy? Don't think so.

• • •

Dinner was surreal. Bernadette was charming. She complimented the house and the yard and everything in between. She said I was "too cute." Could a person be too cute? She was dressed in white. From the tips of her highlighted hair, through the sheer white sweater (Angela whispered, "Prada." I didn't know what this meant), to her stiletto heels (also Prada, apparently), she was a vision in white. I knew she'd be beautiful. I expected that, obviously, because of Angela. Genes don't fall far from the tree.

After a quick call to our favorite chicken place and a hastily thrown-together salad (I now know where the term "tossed salad" comes from) we sat down to dinner.

Cal said, "So, what brings you to town?"

"I've moved here!" said Bernadette.

Cal gulped. (He's got a big Adam's apple — hard to miss.)

Mom shot a glance at Cal. He managed a shrug. "Really? What ... er ... brought that on?"

"I don't know. It was a bit of a lonely Christmas." Bernadette shot a glance at Angela. Angela glanced at me. I looked for Moses.

"We forgot the fries," Angela said. Looked intensely at me.

"Okay." I shrugged.

"Let's get them."

"Okay." I followed her into the kitchen.

As soon as the door closed, she leaned against the counter like she was trying to Heimlich herself.

"You okay?"

Angela straightened immediately. Breathed deeply. "Lonely Christmas?" Breathed again. "Moving here?" Angela grabbed a fry out the box and stuffed it in her mouth.

"Whoa," I said. "Are they making macrobiotic fries now?"

She narrowed her eyes and took another one.

"She seems pretty nice," I said, for something to say.

Angela waved the fry at me. "Oh, no. Do not make that mistake. This is a woman who could make Gandhi reconsider non-violence."

"Okay."

"This is a woman who gave me diet pills for my birthday."

"Were you trying to lose weight?" I asked helpfully.

"I was ten."

As she reached for yet another fry, I took the box from her gently and dumped the contents onto a plate. "Maybe we should get back in there." As much as Serene Angela annoyed me, Unstrung Angela was freaking me out.

Once we were seated at the table, I passed the fries to Bernadette.

"Oh, no. I'm afraid of saturated fats." She smiled.

This made me smile, out of reflex, but also because Bernadette didn't give the impression of being afraid of anything. Especially of wine, as it turned out, as Cal jumped to fill her glass.

"I think I just missed my daughter," she said to my

mother. "And I thought, if the mountain won't come to Mohammed, well ...?"

Angela looked down at her plate. It had been empty, but she grabbed the fries and tumbled an avalanche onto it and asked for the ketchup.

"Oh, honey, really? What would Jenny say?" Bernadette smiled.

Angela didn't answer. Possibly because she'd stuffed a handful of fries in her mouth.

"Jenny?" I asked, still reeling from the sight of Angela with a fry hanging from her lips like a cigarette.

"Jenny Craig. One of our many mother/daughter ventures." Bernadette's smile disappeared for the first time. Without the display of perfectly interlocked white enamel, she looked like an ice sculpture. Her eyes darted around the room, taking everything in. And then, like a magic trick, the smile returned and she was human-ish again. "Angela was going through a chubby phase."

"It's called puberty, Mother," Angela muttered, taking a piece of chicken from the platter. "Some of us went through it."

Bernadette didn't take her eyes off Angela ripping into the drumstick like she'd just been rescued from a desert island. The room was silent.

"Chicken?" I said, passing the platter to Bernadette, whose plate was covered only in green.

"Oh. Thank you. Aren't you polite?" She plucked the smallest piece onto her plate. Almost immediately she removed the skin. Then she looked at it like she wasn't sure what should come next. "So, what do you do, dear?"

She was looking at me. "Um ..."

"She's a kid, Mom. What do you think she does? She goes to school."

"I meant what are her interests?"

"Her interests include going to school."

I was actually pretty happy to just be a "her" in this situation, largely because I suddenly couldn't think of one single interest. I was starting to see why Angela was so unnerved.

"I don't think we need that tone, dear." Bernadette said, cutting a sliver of chicken and placing it in her mouth.

"Normally we try to have well-balanced meals," said Mom quickly. I could see that she was coming to the rescue. Go Mom.

"But you don't have to worry about overeating now," Bernadette said, aiming her gaze at my mother's protruding stomach. "When I was pregnant with Angela I ate like there was no tomorrow."

"I was meaning to tell you about it — the pregnancy," said Cal.

Bernadette waved her manicured hands in the air. "The ex is always the last to know." Then she laughed.

Here's the weird/weirder part: we laughed along

with her. But even as I was laughing I was wondering to myself, Where's the joke?

Angela wasn't laughing. She was inhaling the chicken — skin and all. "I wrote you about it," she said, but it came out kind of muffled. (Probably due to the saturated animal fats.) It was at this moment that I remembered that Angela was a vegetarian. (I didn't say a word. Way to go, me.)

"Really?" Bernadette asked. She cut another infinitesimal piece of chicken breast. "I don't remember."

At this point the phone rang. Cal sprang from the chair like he'd been double bounced off a trampoline. "I'll get it."

It was one of his biking buddies asking if he wanted to go for a ride. He looked hopefully at my mother.

My mom smiled. (A smile not unlike Bernadette's.) "But we have company, Sweetie."

Cal declined reluctantly and hung up the phone. The emphasis on "Sweetie" might have been a deciding factor.

The charm grew a little thin at this point. We all concentrated on our food until Bernadette excused herself to have a cigarette on the patio. As soon as she was out of the room, Mom started piling the plates with gusto. Too much gusto. A chip of porcelain flew across the table.

"I'll help you," Cal said.

"Thanks. That'd be great."

I chewed on one last drumstick, enjoying it immensely. "So," I said to Angela, "you were chubby?"

"Puberty," Angela muttered, rising from her chair. "We better have some fruit around here. She'll die without fruit."

I finished off my chicken and watched Bernadette through the patio doors. She looked impossibly frail, wraithlike. I sucked in my stomach and looked down. Quite a ways from a wraith.

"What are you doing?" Mom demanded as she entered the room. She was carrying cups and a carafe of coffee.

"Trying to imagine skinny."

"You're perfect the way you are," she said with determination.

I smiled at this, suddenly grateful for a mother who served fried foods. "How are you doing?"

"It's fine."

"Yeah, you seem fine."

She smiled at this and I smiled back. For a second it was like we were sharing a how-did-we-end-up-on-Mars joke.

The patio door screeched open and Bernadette re-entered the biosphere. As she struggled to close the door, my mom said, "Cal's been meaning to give that some oil."

"Yes," Bernadette said. "He's good at that." She smiled again.

I promised to write a book on smiles one day. *The Many Uses of the Upturned Lip*, I might call it. She sat down and we all took turns upturning at one another. It was becoming painful by the time Cal and Angela returned. Cal was carrying a pie; Angela brought a plate of fruit.

"Coffee?" said Mom.

"No, thank you," said Bernadette. "I won't sleep if I do." She played with her wine glass and Cal filled it. I thought my mother looked longingly at the glass.

"Fruit?" said Angela.

"Oh, Sweetheart," Bernadette said. I had been thinking about excusing myself from the table when I noticed that her eyes were glistening with tears. This was better than television. "You remembered how much I love fruit."

"It's just a melon, Mom." Angela sat down and, when I thought things couldn't get weirder, helped herself to a huge slab of pie.

"Honey," Bernadette said. "Are you sure?"

Angela looked at her. "No, I'm not. What's chocolate cream pie without extra whipped cream? I'll be right back." She left the room.

"She's a little high-strung," Bernadette explained. "I hope she hasn't been any trouble for you."

"Oh, no," Mom said. "She's delightful. It's been an adjustment, of course, for all of us."

"Of course."

I was on chapter twelve of my book of smiles

when Angela returned with a can of whipped cream. She plunked herself down and proceeded to spray half the can onto her pie. She grinned as she picked up her fork. It was one upturn too many.

"I have homework to do," I said. It had just gotten, officially, too weird.

• • •

"Who's the puppy?" Dell cooed.

I held Moses up to the receiver. I was really getting tired of this routine.

"Who's the puppy-wuppy? Who's the puppiest? Who's the puppers?"

I took the receiver away from his ear. "I'm the puppers," I said in a low, growly voice. "Woof," I added, to make it more believable.

"That's not how he talks." Dell actually sounded indignant.

"Listen. Angela's mom showed up tonight."

There was a pause. "Is she gorgeous?" There was not even a tinge of puppy-wuppers in her tone.

"What do you think?"

Another pause, and then a growl — from Dell, not Moses.

"She's not only gorgeous, she's like ... droid gorgeous. Like science-fiction, take-over-the-world, bullets-shooting-out-of-her-breasts gorgeous."

"Is she prettier than Angela?"

I thought about this. "She might be."

"Whoa. That's something."

"Not exactly prettier. Just ... more. It's like she's been smoothed out, like when you put a hot knife over peanut butter. And her lips are, I don't know. I really can't describe them."

"The Perpetual Pout?"

"There you go."

"She's had work," Dell said knowingly.

"And her teeth? I can't even describe the teeth. It's like some dentist said, 'And you shall be my greatest creation.'"

"So why is this making you so happy?"

"Huh." I moved the receiver to my other ear. "I don't know. It's like Angela has been out-Angela-ed."

"That makes sense. Me, on the other hand, I'm over Angela-ed. Are you coming to the party?"

"You are so determined."

"I want you to come."

"I'll ... pretend to think about it."

"I miss peanut butter."

After her protracted good-bye to Moses, we hung up. I felt bad about the party, but I couldn't see myself going. I tried to imagine it. I did. I tried to imagine myself getting ready and going out the door, and then I saw myself turning around and coming right back inside. I couldn't ask Sam. It would be like we were a couple, and we weren't a couple. And because we weren't a couple, obviously he'd be available and there would be all these girls there. Other girls. Why shouldn't he go out with other girls? No reason. It's not like I thought he should be a monk. Monks have to get that stupid haircut and Sam has such good hair.

And I couldn't go alone. Dell would say that we were going together, but I'd be alone in the back of Marshall's car. We'd walk into the party together and then Marshall would grunt something about getting us a drink, but he'd probably only bring something for Dell. And then I'd probably say something stupid like, *Am I a camel? I don't need to drink?* Marshall would mutter something unintelligible and then Dell would be upset. And there we'd be. Happy New Year's.

Well, I'd thought about it. Done. I sat on my bed and looked at my covered mirror and thought what a relief it was not to have to deal with a reflection. I was just thinking about how simple this made life when there was a knock at my door.

"Come in," I said.

Angela sat down on my chair before she realized it was covered in clothes. She stood up, brushed the clothes off and sat back down again. I waited for a discouraging word about the mess. Nothing.

"How's it going?" I said because somebody had to say something and she was just sitting there gaping.

"Why is she here?" she asked.

I shrugged.

"Seriously, why is she here?"

I shrugged more seriously.

"She wants something. She always wants something. The woman has never thought about anybody other than herself in the entire time that she's been on this earth. Which is forty years, by the way. Not that I'm allowed to say that. Oh, no. She's the last woman who still lies about her age. Did you know that when I was eight years old she went out with my soccer coach?"

"What?"

"She told him that I had a weak bladder."

"Do you?"

"That's not the point. Why would she tell him that? And I don't have a weak bladder ... anymore. And then she went out with my ninth-grade English teacher. Who I had a crush on."

"Well, it probably wouldn't have worked out between the two of you," I said. Angela glared at me. "But that's not the point."

"It's like as soon as I was born she's all competitive. She used to compare our baby pictures. Who does that? 'Too bad you didn't get my mouth,' she said. 'Leading ladies have big mouths.'"

I laughed.

"What's funny?"

I stopped. "Nothing. She wants you to be a leading lady?"

"Well, she didn't make it, did she? It would be the next best thing, I guess. Who can figure her out? Anyway, she knows that I don't want to be a movie star."

I risked it. "I thought you did want to be a movie star."

"I want to be an actor."

"Okay," I said, unsure of the difference.

She stood up and, out of reflex, turned to the mirror. "Why can't I see myself?"

Oh, I almost felt sorry that my mother wasn't here for this question. She would have had such a good time saying "Ah, why *can't* you see yourself?"

Before I could explain my so-called psychology experiment, she said, "I feel so ugly when I'm around her."

"You're not ugly."

"I'm not looking for a compliment. I just feel full of ugliness when I'm around her, like it's in my blood."

That's when it stopped being fun and I felt a very unusual thing. I felt sorry for her.

"This ... this stuff ..." she waved her arms around and I wondered if she was talking about my messy room. "The stuff I just said, that's nothing." She shook her head. "*She's* in me. Her ugliness is in me and it all comes out when she's around. And now she's here."

"So is Cal," I said, suddenly feeling so out of my depth that I wanted to call my mother for reinforcements.

"Him? The guy who left?" She suddenly put her hands on her stomach and turned a yellowish color.

"Are you okay?"

"I feel sick."

"Could it be the four pieces of chicken or maybe the can of whipped cream?"

But Angela didn't seem to hear me. "She will not make me throw up. She will not. She will not."

And with that, she left the room.

I was almost tempted to take the blanket off the mirror because I suddenly needed a second opinion. I was pretty sure, although not certain, that I'd just seen the real Angela and she was far from perfect. She was scarred.

I fell asleep to the sound of vacuuming.

Chapter Sixteen

Moses and I fell into a routine pretty quick. He would whimper when I put him in the basket beside my bed, where he remained until my mom came in to say good night, after which I would pick him up and let him snuggle beside me. He wasn't getting any prettier, but he was a good snuggler. Every once in a while he'd push his head beside mine and lick me on the cheek. Not a big accomplishment considering that his tongue was always available. Then, at about six or seven in the morning, he'd whimper again, only with more intensity, and I'd take him outside to do his little doggy business. He always gave me a baleful look when he saw the snow. I'd tell him that this was just the way life was.

"Every day, Moses, every day. You know the drill." I gave his rotund hindquarters a little shove. He tipped over and skidded on his nose. I laughed. "That's probably how you got your scrunched face in the first place." I picked him up and gave him a little cuddle then put him down again. "You can do this. I believe in you, Mr. Puppy Wupperson."

"I'm going to have to report that to Dell," came a voice behind me.

I turned around, startled. It was Sam, walking across the backyard, leaving a trail of footprints in the newly fallen snow.

"I'll deny it."

"What kind of dog is he anyway?"

I shrugged. "A crossbreed. A little bit of bulldog, I think, and terrier. Maybe some Lhaso Apso. He's quite exotic, don't you think?"

"A mutt."

"Yeah."

"Mutts are good."

I smiled. "Good job."

Sam looked surprised.

I pointed to Moses. "He pooped."

"Way to go, Moses. Nice one."

I laughed. "You don't have to go that far."

He smiled, and then the iceberg floated in and planted itself on my chest. It was the smile that did it.

"So, that party tonight?" He ran his hand through his already disheveled hair.

"Yeah."

"That would be a bad idea, right?"

"The worst."

"Okay, then."

A gust of arctic air blew across the yard and my quilt slipped off my shoulder. Sam reached over to grab it, but I reached it before he did and tucked myself neatly inside.

"Sorry," he said. "I didn't mean that in a *sexual* way. I know you don't believe in teenage sex."

I looked away, embarrassed.

"And I didn't come over here to ..." He shook his messy, bedroom hair. "I wasn't asking you to the party."

"I know."

He held out two cups. "My mom needs to borrow some sugar and flour. She's making pancakes." He walked over to the door and knocked.

"Shh," I said. "Nobody's awake yet. I'll get it."

"Don't worry about it." He turned to leave.

"Do you need it or not?"

"Whatever."

He followed me into the house, where I realized that I had been wrong about the sleeping household. Angela was at the table reading the newspaper. Mari ... whatever was nestled comfortably in her lap. Sam wandered over and sat down like he'd been invited. "Nice cat," he said.

"Do you want to hold him?" She held out the kitten, not giving Sam much choice. This was not the Angela with a face full of fries. This was the Angela who woke up ready for her Cover Girl shoot.

I slammed a door as I looked for the flour and sugar. Who baked around here, anyway? Nobody.

"Shh," said Angela, putting a finger up to her

glossed lips. Lip gloss in the morning. That's all I'm saying.

"What's his name?" asked Sam.

"I thought it was a she," I said, but nobody was listening. Sam was petting the kitten like it was the first kitten he'd ever laid eyes on.

"Mahatma," Angela said.

"As in Gandhi?"

"I figured we could use a little peace around here."

"Cool," he said, still petting away like a madman.

I dumped sugar into the cup. "Well, Moses wandered in the desert for forty years." They both looked at me. I poured the flour into the cup too quickly; it spilled like an avalanche over the countertop. I scooped at it and put most of it back. Not a difficult job unless you're trying to hold a quilt around you at the same time. And then my hair fell in my face so that I couldn't see, so I dropped the quilt and pushed the hair away. By now all I could think was, Why the pig pajamas? Why, today, the pig pajamas?

I shoved the cups across the counter. "Here."

Sam got up and took them. "Thanks for the food. Cuz you always need food, right?"

As he opened the door I called after him, "I'm just going to go upstairs and turn on my lamp."

He paused at the door and looked concerned. "I hope you don't mean that in a *sexual* way." And then he left.

Angela sat there looking amused. "He really is pretty cute, isn't he?"

I scrubbed at the flour, which turned to a pasty glop in the dishrag.

"It would help if you got rid of most of it first and then tried to wash the counter."

"I think I know how to clean a counter."

"I don't think you do. You know how to make the mess. I just don't think you know how to clean up the mess."

Spiteful little witch, I thought. But I just continued to push around the mounds of glue.

"Take Sam, for instance. Now there's a mess."

"You take Sam, if you want him." Where did that come from?

She returned to reading her paper. "Well, he likes you, for one thing. And for another thing, I'm through with men."

"You're through with men?" It would be like a pie shell being through with fruit.

"Yep."

"Why?"

"Because men are pigs."

"Men are not pigs," I said. "My dad is not a pig. Cal is not a pig. The Prime Minister of Canada is not a pig." Did I know the prime minister? Maybe he was. "Mahatma Gandhi was not a pig," I added triumphantly.

She crooked her head. "I'll give you that one. But he was celibate and he's dead, so ..."

I continued scrubbing. Angela gave a groan and pushed away from the table. She walked over to the drawer and pulled out a spatula. She scraped the congealing glop into her hand and calmly dropped it in the garbage can. Then she took a clean dishcloth and expertly wiped every streak until it shone. "There," she said happily.

"You didn't exactly seem opposed to pigs when you were going out with Sam and Marshall at the same time last summer." This little gem just sort of dropped out of my mouth.

Angela dried her hands and scooped Mahatma into her arms. She held him close. I was about to admit I'd crossed a line when she said, "Sam isn't. Marshall is. You might want to warn Dell about him." She turned at the doorway. "Nice jammies, by the way. And you have flour all over your face. Very alluring."

Well, that wasn't so zen, was it? I felt a little twitch of accomplishment. Mostly I felt like I needed a shower.

• • •

Dell called later that afternoon, making her final plea for me to go to the party.

"It's going to be fun. I promise," she pleaded.

"You'll have fun without me. It's actually possible.

You are a confident, mature, beautiful woman."

"What?"

"Nothing."

"But it's New Year's. It won't be right to greet the new year without you. We always spend New Year's together."

"That was when we were both losers without boyfriends." Blurtation.

A pause. "You're not a loser."

"I know. I am a confident, mature, beautiful woman."

"Stop saying that. It's creepy. Just come, okay?" She almost sounded desperate.

"Why do you want me there so much, Dell? What's up?"

"Nothing. Let me talk to Moses."

"What's up?" I repeated.

"Things are just getting so intense, you know?"

I didn't.

"Not bad intense ... just intense, intense. And if you're there, it'll be fun."

"You want me to be buffer girl?"

"It's not that," she said, but it wasn't convincing.

I hesitated about telling her what Angela had said about Marshall. Angela wasn't on the top of her list of most credible witnesses. "You know, maybe you should listen to your gut."

"My gut is fine."

"It's just that, well, Angela ..."

"Yes?"

"She said that I should warn you about Marshall."

"What?" She sounded indignant. "What did she say?"

"Just that. Like, you should watch out."

"I'm going to take advice to the lovelorn from the Ice Queen? That's what Marshall calls her. That's what everybody calls her." Her voice was brittle.

"Marshall and I have something special, Jes. Why does nobody understand that? Why don't you understand that?"

"Then why don't you want to go to the party with him?"

"Well, excuse me for wanting to include you."

"That's what this is about? You feel sorry for me?"

"No. That's not what I said."

"I have Moses."

I heard her sigh. "Okay. Put him on." I heard her tell Moses that she loved him with all her heart and that he was the best puppy ever and that he would grow into his looks. Then she said Happy New Year. I said Happy New Year in my gruff, puppy voice and she giggled. So it ended okay.

• • •

"You have enough food?" Mom asked as she hovered around the door with Cal. They were going to a party at Bernadette's condo. A combination housewarming and New Year's. It was a theme party: Arabian nights. Angela said it was because her mother had a fabulous belly-dancing costume. My mother's mouth had grown quite stern, but she'd coaxed a smile out of it and said that she'd just go as herself: a big, fat preggo.

"Snacks, galore," I said, lounging on the couch. I was actually looking forward to the evening. I had Cheesies and pop and ice cream and Moses, plus a couple of old movies and my freshly laundered pig PJs. I was ready to party hard. There was a slight setback when I realized that Angela would be joining me.

"You're not going to the party?" I had asked. According to Dell, *everybody* was going and Angela was certainly *everybody* by now.

"So I can get pawed by a drunken lout?" She said this like it was inevitable.

"So everyone there will be a lout?" I was feeling a little indignant. I'd never come close to being pawed.

"Pigs and louts. Pretty much."

My mother watched us, wistfully it seemed. "Are you sure you don't need some company? I don't mind staying. Right, Cal? We could stay."

"Oh, definitely," he said, almost eagerly.

I laughed. "No. You'll really have a good time. This is very twenty-first century of you guys, partying with the ex." I almost gave her the blended family speech, but she suddenly looked a little mournful. "You can stay, if you want. You don't always have to be mature."

She drew herself up at this. "Don't be silly," she said. "I just thought you might need me." Good old

Mom. Good old pregnant, big-as-a-pony Mom.

"Okay, then. Have fun, kids," I said.

"Well, of course we'll have fun," she said. "Right, Cal?"

Cal nodded. "Sure."

"That sounded convincing," she said. "Listen, if you don't want to go, we don't have to go."

"You don't have to go," I reminded her.

"I want to go. It's not that I don't want to go." But she still wasn't moving. "Are you sure you'll be all right? You have the numbers?"

"Yes, your cell and Cal's cell and Bernadette's home *and* cell. Paramedics, police, fire department, in case Moses has a seizure."

She smiled weakly.

"You look really pretty, Mom," I finally said. "You might want to wipe the lipstick off your teeth, though."

She spun around quicker than I would have thought possible in her present condition and stared at herself in the hall mirror. She examined her teeth, which were white and glistening, lipstick-free. "You're pure evil," she said.

"Well, that's my job."

Cal opened the door a crack. "I guess we should get going." He walked out like he was heading to the electric chair.

"And make sure that dog doesn't poop —" Mom added.

"Hey, a dog's gotta poop."

"— in the house." But she smiled. "Happy New Year, Sweetie." She waved to Angela. "Happy New Year, Angela."

"Thanks. You, too."

Once they were gone, I tucked myself into my quilt and picked up the remote control. "Yeah, they're gonna have fun."

Angela was looking at me with a strange expression on her face.

"What?" I said, automatically running my tongue across my teeth for Cheesie bits.

"You and your mom."

"What about it?"

She shook her head. "Nothing. Turn up the volume, will you?" She sat there for a second, stroking Mahatma, looking more than a little like Dr. Evil. Then she turned to me. "You want a beer?"

I looked wistfully at my two-liter bottle of pop. "Okay."

She went to the kitchen and brought back two bottles. No opener. "Never mind," she said. She held a bottle up to her mouth and neatly removed the cap with her even, white teeth.

"Wow," I said. "Very skanky."

"Thank you," she said. "I learned from the best."

• • •

At eleven o'clock the phone rang. I jumped up, then sat down again, a little woozy. Angela, I noticed, had barely touched her beer. Too many calories, I guess. The phone rang again.

Looking amused, Angela said, "I'll get it."

It was probably my mother. I practiced saying, "We're fine," hoping I didn't sound drunk. I didn't. But when Angela brought the phone to me, it was Dell.

"Hey," she said. "Happy Almost New Year." The sound in the background was deafening.

"Same to you. Are you having fun?"

"Am I what?"

I yelled into the phone. "Are you having fun?"

"No, I'm having fun," she yelled back.

"Okay."

"Let me talk to Moses," she said. Except she tried it three times and every time she had trouble pronouncing Moses. It sounded more like Moshez. Then she gave up. "Put the little bastard on."

"Are you drunk?" I yelled.

"No. I just had ... no. I'm good. I'm fun. My legs don't work, though."

"Are you okay?"

"I'm relaxed. I'm fun."

But before I could put Moses on the line, she hung up. I sat there looking at the receiver. "Well, that was weird."

"She's having a good time?" Angela asked, nibbling delicately at a pretzel. I think she'd been working on that one all evening.

"I guess so. She sounded strange."

"Is she drinking?"

"Maybe. She doesn't really drink, though." I shrugged, looking at my empty beer bottle. "But you never know. She said her legs didn't work."

Angela sat up at this. "What did she say ... exactly?"

"She said, 'My legs don't work.'"

"Anything else?"

"Why?"

"Was she speaking clearly?"

I looked down at Moses, who was nestled in comfortably for the night. "Moshez," I said. "She said she was relaxed."

Angela was on her feet and she was pacing.

"What's wrong with you?"

"It might be nothing."

"What might be nothing?"

She stopped pacing. "Do you want to go to a party?"

• • •

Angela was a careful driver. As I watched the still-lit houses pass by in a lazy blur, I was grateful for this because she didn't have her license, so it wasn't really a given. I was also still unclear as to why we were going — me in my pig pajamas — to a party. She hadn't given me a chance to get dressed. She had suddenly turned urgent as we looked for the keys to Cal's car.

But now I needed some clarification. "Why are we doing this again?"

"Okay, I could be wrong, but it sounds like she's had a roofie."

"Huh?"

"Rohypnol."

I still needed clarification.

"The date-rape drug."

My heart stood still. Sometimes it's fear that will do that to you and sometimes it's a kind of knowing. This was both.

Chapter Seventeen

We checked the numbers on the houses against the address that Angela had scribbled down, until we turned a corner and pulled up in front of a brightly lit house with people spilling out onto the sidewalk.

We passed a boy throwing up in the bushes; my pig pajamas narrowly missed being hit by something that reminded me of my father's Christmas curry.

"Hey, Angela," he said, wiping his mouth with his shirt.

"Hey, Justin." She kept her distance. "Have you seen Marshall and Dell?"

He shook his head and his face suddenly turned gray. He pivoted and hurled into the bushes.

"No problem," she said calmly. "We'll find them."

Meekly, I followed Angela as she moved purposefully through the house. We passed a curved staircase and a very passionate couple. I couldn't see their faces so I leaned in to take a closer look.

"Do you mind?" said the girl.

"Do you want to join us?" said the boy.

"My mistake," I said.

Angela pulled me through the throng that was pulsing to the music like one large intestine.

"Do you know where you're going?" I yelled above the noise.

We looked in the kitchen and interrupted two more entwined couples. "There seems to be a theme going on here," I said.

"What?"

"Nothing."

"Maybe we should split up."

"Oh please no," I said.

"Let's try upstairs," she said.

So we walked past the passionate couple again—this time they didn't even look up—and started opening bedroom doors. People in various states of undress yelled for us to leave.

"What now?" I asked.

Angela stood with her hands on her hips.

"Maybe they left?" I suggested.

"Nobody leaves a New Year's party before midnight," she said matter-of-factly.

"Yeah," I said, like I knew.

"Basement," she suddenly said. "Maybe there's a basement."

So we trudged back down the stairs, past the couple who were probably deciding what to name their first child. Angela spotted the door to the basement like she had a fair amount of experience scouting out-of-the-way locations. She squeezed through the crowd and disappeared down the stairs. A girl with long, black hair pushed in front of me, giggling, pulling a shaggy-haired boy in her wake.

"Jes?"

"Sam?"

The girl glared at me. I glared back.

"What are you doing here?" Sam asked.

"I was invited," I said inexplicably.

"You're wearing your pajamas."

The stupid girl giggled. Well, I had no idea if she was stupid, but she giggled stupidly. "Nice pigs," she said.

I pushed past Sam and into the stairwell. He called my name, but I kept going. At the bottom of the stairs I looked around, trying to get my bearings. Then I saw Angela's long, blond hair disappearing into a corner room. When I entered the room I saw her kneeling beside a bed. I heard her say, "What did you give her?" to Marshall, who got up awkwardly and managed to look indignant.

"Nothing," he said, doing up the button of his shirt. "She had a couple of drinks."

"What did you give her?" Angela repeated, looking around the room. She pointed to a glass that was half full of blue liquid. "What's in that?"

"There's stuff floating around. How should I know?"

"Pig," she muttered.

I felt my legs go weak and I thought I was going

to fall. I sat down on a chair and watched as Angela pulled Dell to a sitting position. She looked like a confused, disoriented ghost. I couldn't move. What was I doing, sitting here?

But Angela looked like she knew exactly what she was doing. "Dell, can you throw up?" she asked. "Can you?"

Dell actually smiled at this, a goofy, dopey smile. "Sure." She looked like a little kid with the right answer.

Angela pulled Dell's legs over the side of the bed and then my own started working. I jumped up to help her.

"There's a bathroom in the hallway," Angela said.

"Hey, Jes, you came." Dell smiled stupidly up at me as we hauled her to the bathroom.

Marshall followed us and stood in the doorway.

"What did you do to her, Marshall?" My voice was shaking.

"Nothing," he said. And then he smiled.

All I could hear was the thud of my heart against the wall of my chest and a thin, piercing ringing in my ears. I swung. I think I grazed his smug face, but he stepped aside. I went hurtling into the hall. I struggled to my feet, preparing to take another swing, but somebody held me back. It was Sam.

"Jes, calm down. What's going on?" he asked.

"Let me go," I said, struggling, but he held me

firm. Marshall pushed past us and was gone. I could see Dell now, bent over the toilet, throwing up. Angela was holding her hair.

"That's good, honey. Let it go," she said gently.

I slumped against the wall. My eyes burned with frustrated tears.

When Dell was finished, she looked surprised to see Angela beside her. She pushed her away and staggered toward me. I grabbed her as she lurched forward.

"I'm so embarrassed," she whispered into my hair.

"No," I whispered back. I felt bad that Dell had pushed Angela, but I didn't know what to say. I tried to give her a look that would say that Dell didn't know what she was doing. But Angela's gentle face had slid behind perfection.

She looked in the mirror and fixed her hair. "Yeah, well, this party blows. Let's get her home."

"I'll come with you," Sam said.

I shook my head. "Stay. Enjoy yourself." I knew I shouldn't have said that. I knew it and I said it anyway.

• • •

Outside, the air felt raw, like it was scraping my skin. I pulled off my jacket and wrapped it around Dell. I helped her into the back seat of the car. By now we'd drawn a crowd. I could see Sam holding people back and telling them to go into the house. I didn't check to see if he watched as the car pulled away.

We didn't say anything all the way to Dell's house. When we pulled into her driveway, I turned to her. "Are you okay?"

She looked better, but her voice was small. "Yes."

"Are your parents home?"

She nodded.

"I'll help you to the door."

"No," she said, her voice more forceful. "I don't want them asking any questions."

I got out of the car anyway and opened the back door. Dell slid out without a word to Angela. "Just let me walk you to the door," I said.

She shook her head. "No."

"You are so stubborn! What if you fall in the bushes and we don't find you till spring." I tried to be funny because I was all out of anything else.

Her eyes were dark and smudged with makeup. She pulled my coat around her. I shivered. "Oh, God, your coat," she said, taking it off.

Angela barked, "Don't let her take off the coat. She might be in shock." She got out of the car, grabbed Dell, not very gently, and marched her up the sidewalk. "Get right into bed. If there isn't a message on the phone by the time we get home with you singing the alphabet song, we're coming back. Do you understand that?"

Dell nodded, eyes wide.

"You," she said to me gruffly. "Back in the car."

I gave Dell a quick hug and she shuffled up the sidewalk and into the house. Shivering, I slipped into the front seat. Angela gunned the motor.

After a few minutes I said, "The alphabet song?"

Her shoulders lost some of their determined stiffness. "I just want to make sure that she's thinking straight."

"Maybe we should have taken her to the hospital?" I said. "Maybe we should go back and talk to her mom and dad." I felt so lost, so stupid, so completely out of my depth.

"She's talking coherently and it didn't look like she had that much."

"But still —"

"We don't have to," she said. "I never did."

It took a couple of seconds for the words to settle in. "You never had to what?"

"Go to the hospital. She just needs to sleep it off."

"When did you never have to go to the hospital?"

There was a pause. "Never."

"But you said ..."

"Nothing. I said nothing. It's under control."

"Okay. Let's just go home."

"We will," she said. "I have to make a stop."

• • •

I waited in the car as Angela went into an all-night drugstore. Vaguely, I wondered if she was going to hold it up. It seemed the direction this evening was taking.

I was imagining her stealing their complete line of makeup with a comb in her pocket for a gun. I was imagining being on the lam with her for the rest of our lives. Maybe doing a Thelma-and-Louise off a cliff. Nothing seemed impossible.

And then she was driving again.

I didn't ask where we were going and, when we pulled up to a house, I wasn't surprised at where we were. Marshall's car was in the driveway.

"Okay," she said, grabbing the drugstore bag. She pulled out a thick, black marker. She stuffed it into her pocket and began to rummage through the glove box.

I raised my hand timidly. "Question?"

"Aha," she said.

"Aha, what?"

"Cal is completely predictable." She pulled out a heavy-duty flashlight. Then she grinned. "Are you coming?"

"Murff," I said. That's puppy for "oh, crap."

"Well?"

"Well, what are we doing?"

"We are setting a wrong right."

"I support the idea, but the lights are on." I pointed to the house. "He must have just gotten home."

"I suspect he went straight to bed to pass out. Or maybe he passed out in the hallway. Who knows, who cares? Where's your sense of justice, not to mention adventure?"

I refrained from mentioning that the last adventure we had together was last summer when she and I were dragged into the security office at the mall because of a necklace *she* had planted in my knapsack and that maybe, just maybe, I had a few trust issues. I refrained because this was for Dell.

Stealthily, I followed her into the night. The air didn't feel raw anymore. It felt dangerous and a little bit right, almost approving. She shoved the flashlight into my hand and told me where to shine it. Then, with total calm, she began to write large, neat letters on the trunk of his car. At least, that's where she started. When she finished writing, she was at the front where she added two exclamation marks to her message.

She stepped out of the way. The band of light shook as I pointed it. I read what she'd written: I HAVE TO DRUG GIRLS BEFORE THEY'LL HAVE SEX WITH ME!!

"Well, that's permanent," I finally said.

"You do the crime, you do the time," she said. Then she took out her keys and scratched a solid line around the circumference of the car. The red paint gave way easily. She stood back to admire her work. "So, we're done?"

I nodded. "I think we are."

• • •

Thankfully, Mom and Cal weren't home yet. But then, as Angela said, nobody leaves a New Year's party before midnight. Exhaustion seemed to hit us at the same time and we stumbled up the stairs to our rooms. The first thing I did was check the voice mail. One new message. Dell's voice sang the alphabet song faintly. I put the receiver down, relieved.

Moses had tucked himself neatly into bed. I guess he'd mastered the art of jumping while I was gone. "Clever boy," I said, crawling in beside him. I picked him up and cradled him in my arms. He dragged his chubby tongue across my cheek.

I tried to fall asleep, but the adrenaline was still pumping away. The clock shone red at me: 11:55. Almost a new year.

I couldn't stay still. It suddenly seemed like such a caper. Me, I'd been involved in a caper. I needed to talk about it. I pushed the covers off and got out of bed. I was about to knock on Angela's door when I heard the front door open.

"Jessica? Are you home?"

When I reached the landing and looked downstairs, I saw my mother holding my empty bottle of beer. She peered up at me. "Why is the car warm?"

Chapter Eighteen

Here's a way not to start a new year. Your pregnant mother is holding an empty bottle of your beer when you've only recently returned, freshly feloned, from committing a crime.

"Would you come down here, please?"

I was impressed with her "please."

"And would you ask Angela to come down as well?"

"I'd be happy to," I said. Happy to buy time. Happy to fix an alibi, make a plan, jump out the window.

I burst into Angela's room. She was sitting cross-legged on the floor. Her groovy sitar music was playing softly. "Hey, Happy New Year and the fuzz is here."

"The what? What are you talking about?"

I closed the door behind me. "Our parents. My parent and your parent. Our collective parents."

"They're home already?"

"Seems nobody told them about the party-till-midnight rule, and they want to know why the car is warm."

"Well, crap."

It was vaguely comforting to see a look of concern

cross her face. But then it wasn't comforting. I needed her calm, cool, appraising criminal mind working for us. "Snap out of it," I said. "What are we going to tell them?"

She unfolded herself gracefully. "Calm down."

"I am calm.'"

"You're practically hysterical. Breathe."

I gave her that one. I took a breath. It was more of a rasp. "What, what, what are we going to tell them?"

"That we went to the drugstore." She shook her shimmery hair at me. "Have you learned nothing from me?"

I thought about it. "We *did* go to the drugstore. That's good."

"Exactly. It's the truth."

"It's brilliant. You're brilliant."

She put her hands on my shoulders. "Just leave the talking to me, okay? You blurt things."

I followed her out the door. "I am a blurter."

• • •

I blurted in ten seconds. This is how it went down.

Mom asked, serenely, why the car engine was warm. Cal stood beside her, nodding like a bobble-head. Angela said that we needed to go to the drugstore. Mom asked why. Angela said I needed tampons. I was in the middle of thinking how brilliant this was and how nobody ever questions that when my mom said didn't I have my period just last week?

That's when I caved. Just started spewing information

like somebody dialed 411 and I was the only operator left on earth. I rattled off names, dates and times, possible motives and influences and distinguishing birthmarks. I heard myself chattering and I was shouting, *Shut up! Shut up!* inside my head, but I couldn't stop; my internal brakes were busted. "So, you see," I concluded. "We had no choice."

"And you were drinking?" She held up the bottle again. Exhibit A.

"Just me," I said.

Angela just looked at me as if to say thanks for nothing.

"Do Dell's parents know?"

"No, she didn't want us to tell them. She's fine. She called and sang."

"She sang?"

This sounded less reassuring out loud. I just about pointed a blaming finger at Angela for this one, but I restrained myself.

Mom turned to Cal. "We need to call them."

"Why, why do you need to? I promised Dell that we wouldn't say anything."

Angela snorted at this. It wasn't a particularly delicate sound, but I didn't have time to enjoy it.

"Really, Mom, she's fine."

She held out her hand abruptly. "That's enough from you." She spread the fingers of her hand and began counting off. "Drinking underage. Driving without a license. Car theft, really. Possible assault ...

and vandalism. That's a pretty full night, wouldn't you say? It might be time to go to bed."

"It might be."

Angela followed me to the door of my room instead of disappearing, as I'd hoped, inside hers. "Did you have to tell them everything?"

I shrugged.

"I mean, it was mesmerizing. I couldn't stop watching. It was ..." She stood with her hands outstretched.

"Mesmerizing?" I guessed.

"I've never seen anything like it in my life. It's like they'd given you truth serum. No, it's like you voluntarily swallowed an entire bottle. Everything down to the last minute detail. You told them about Justin's puke!"

"Well, it all seemed connected."

"The color of Marshall's car, the brand of felt pen, the way the key sounded, you didn't leave out a single detail."

"But I told them how competent you were at getting Dell to throw up, remember?" I said in a soothing voice. I put my hands on her shoulders and turned her around to face her room. She was still sputtering. "Listen to some music, maybe let the light flow into the vessel of you." I opened the door and she walked inside. I closed it gently behind her.

I was tempted to take the blanket off my mirror to see what a complete idiot looked like. Instead, I listened again to Dell's message. The soft singing calmed me. And then I knew why I'd spilled my guts. I couldn't let there be anything wrong with Dell.

• • •

It took some fast talking the next day to get my mother to let me visit Dell. I think the only reason she agreed was that I'd finally befuddled her. She didn't have a clue how to punish me. And then she got confused about how to punish Angela because there's the whole step situation and apparently the blended family manual is unclear on this point. Cal had gone off for an early morning ride. To clear his head, my mother said, but she didn't seem happy about it. She just sat there rubbing her tummy like it was a Buddha belly and she was looking for answers.

"An hour," she said finally. "No more."

I was out the door, Moses in tow, before she could change her mind. I went the long way to avoid walking past Sam's house. I was fairly sure that he would be just as eager to avoid me, but I wasn't leaving it to chance. Chance was out to get me. What were the odds of my mother coming home before the car had cooled down?

Facing Dell's parents wasn't so bad. They were grateful that my mother had called and I could tell that Dell's mom had been crying. If my mom mentioned the vandalism part, they didn't say anything. Maybe they knew and were even happy about it? Maybe they understood that justice had to be done.

In the bright light of day, I had no regrets. Maybe I even felt a little heroic.

I knocked on Dell's door and heard a quiet, "Go away."

"It's me," I said, pushing the door open.

She was in bed. I let Moses scramble out of my arms. He ran around in two circles and then looked up at me. *What next*, he seemed to be saying. I picked him up and took him over to Dell. Her eyes were swollen and red, still smudged with last night's mascara. I plopped him down on the bed. She reached out and petted him.

"He wanted to see you," I said, prepared to do my Puppy Wupperson voice, but something in her eyes stopped me. "Are you okay?"

She shook her head. "I feel so stupid."

I sat down on the chair beside her bed. "This was his fault, Dell. Have your parents called the police?"

"No."

"Why not?"

"They wouldn't be able to prove anything. He asked me if I wanted something to help me relax and, like an idiot, I said yes. I thought he meant a drink. So that's how stupid I am."

I had to ask. "Did he ... he didn't ..."

"No," she shook her head. "The cavalry arrived in time."

Relief swept over me. "This is his fault," I said again. "Not yours."

She shook her head even more vehemently. "No,

no, it's not, Jes." Her voice sounded strange, empty. "I should have seen it."

"That's just crazy."

"Don't try to make me feel better, Jes. Don't." She was mad. But that was good. A mad Dell was usually a good thing, unless she was mad at me.

"I'm not trying to make you feel better ... or maybe I am. What's wrong with that?"

"What's wrong is ... oh, never mind."

"What are you thinking?" Oh, God, I sounded like my mother. "Tell me what you're thinking."

"I'm thinking that you're smart, Jes."

"Huh?"

"It's like you keep a fence around you, a barbed-wire fence, and you're smart. It's like you have a layer of blubber."

"Gee, thanks."

She shook her head, not smiling. "Oil, then, like ducks have. Or a brick house, like the third pig."

"So, are you on one of your mother's tranquilizers?"

"You know how to protect yourself and you're so, so right. Everybody told me about Marshall. Everybody. My parents, you, even Angela. And I knew it, too. I did." She put a fist on her stomach. "Right here, I knew it. But I kept telling myself it was love." She pressed harder and I could see pain on her face. "I make myself sick."

"Stop it." She was scaring me.

"I didn't see it coming, Jes. I knew it was wrong,

that love isn't like that, but I still couldn't see it. He was pressuring me and ..."

"Dell, please." My eyes were filling up. "Don't talk anymore."

"And now it's all I can see. How awful things are, how awful the world is. How people lie to each other and to themselves because we want things to be beautiful and it's really all ugly. Suffering and hate and slavery and war and how little kids get hurt all the time. All the time, everywhere. And how you felt when your parents got divorced and when your little sister died. I could never feel that and I'm so, so sorry. I'm so sorry."

I held her. I didn't know what else to do because I couldn't tell her that she was wrong except about the barbed-wire fence. I wanted to tell her that I couldn't stand to see her suffering and I couldn't stand not being able to help.

Springtime

Chapter Nineteen

January and February passed quietly; March crept in, sly and soaking. Dell was healing on the outside. She even managed to pass Marshall in the halls at school without going pale. She did her schoolwork, took actual notes and gained a bit of weight. She smiled when something was obviously funny, and even laughed. But it was hollow. She was hollow. And I couldn't fix her.

My dad became inundated with renovation jobs so the wall in our house remained partially torn down. I thought this would drive my mother crazy, but she didn't seem to notice. She was busy at work and busy growing. Every once in a while I wondered if we were planning to put the baby in a box beside the stove. We seemed to have achieved a state of suspended animation. A static family. And we were polite. Oh, my, we were polite. Angela was well on her way to becoming a Buddhist scholar and tried to teach me all about Nirvana and nothingness, or was it everything-ness? She was also very flexible. Cal had achieved a fitness level hitherto unknown by the common man. And I was just going with the flow. Except there was no flow.

Mr. Truelove, however, seemed to be on a steady decline; but at least he was moving. Some days he showed up with two different shoes, sometimes with no socks. One day he brought a CD player to class and played The Beatles. He didn't give a lecture, no notes, nothing. Just sat there and grooved to "Let It Be." Over and over and over. Jumpy Kate finally asked if the CD was stuck. He just pressed the button again.

I looked over to Dell, who shrugged.

Sam and I talked about Dell and that was it. I felt weird about having told him to stay and enjoy the party and I felt weird about the black-haired girl he was with and then I felt weird about feeling weird and that was way too much of that. When we passed each other in the hallway it was like we were on a conveyor belt. Sometimes he said hi, sometimes I said hi. Sometimes we smiled, and then I'd wonder about the black-haired girl again and the thought made my stomach hurt. Usually a muffin or some fries took the pain away, so I knew it was never love in the first place. Just a kind of hunger.

The one person who seemed to be thriving, come to think of it, was Bernadette. She was moving ahead at full speed. She'd started a talent agency. For a mere two hundred bucks and a head shot, she'd send you off to be an extra if there was a movie shooting in town or find somebody to stick you in a catalogue. Angela was her first client. I was surprised that Angela would have anything to do with her, but she just said that a job was a job and she needed the money.

• • •

"Do you think Truelove still wants us to do that extra assignment?" I asked Dell one day on the way to class.

"What extra assignment?"

"The one about life ... and if we're qualified? You know, the save-your-ass assignment."

"Oh, right." She shrugged her still-too-thin shoulders. "I don't know." Then she smiled. "Dare you to ask him."

"Really? You're daring me?" I felt a little surge of hope at this. It was a little old-Dellish.

"A hundred bucks says you don't have the nerve."

"You're lying."

"Five bucks. One. A dollar says you don't have the nerve."

"You're on."

"But you have to say it's the save-your-ass assignment."

"Really?"

"I just made myself a dollar."

"You think you know me, but you don't. I'm very daring, Dell."

"Mm-hmm."

I waited until the end of the class. The bell was

only moments away and Dell had been taunting me the whole time. It seemed so familiar that I felt a rush of bravery. I raised my hand.

He didn't notice so I shook it a little. Jumpy Kate seemed surprised, since I was not exactly known for class participation. Finally Dell said, "I think Jes has a question."

When he looked at me I suddenly realized that we hadn't even made eye contact since the Christmas Eve debacle. Why, I asked myself, was I doing this again?

"Yes, Jes?"

"Hey, that rhymes," yelled Troy, obviously dying for some action in a class that had gotten predictably predictable.

"You, to the principal's office," said Mr. Truelove.

"What? Are you serious?"

Mr. Truelove turned only marginally toward him. "Now." It was only one word, but it was the way he said it that was impressive — drill-sergeant serious.

I tried to remember how he looked when he'd stood at my dad's doorway saying *God bless us, everyone*, but I couldn't. "I was just wondering about that extra assignment."

"What are you talking about?"

"Er, that assignment about life."

Dell looked at me sideways, eyebrows raised as far as they would go.

"The extra one, the ... er ... save-your-ass assignment?" I mumbled.

"What was that?"

"The save-your-ass assignment." As soon as I said the words, I kind of regretted it. Especially since Flynn tittered with appreciation.

He silenced Flynn with a glower and moved a step closer. "Refresh me."

"Well, I think it had to do with recording the things that show how we want to be in the world more than just ..."

Flynn made an obnoxious sucking noise.

"You, join your juvenile delinquent friend in the principal's office."

Flynn sputtered.

"Now."

Flynn left.

"Continue," he said.

"Never mind."

"Continue."

"It was just about how we want to take up the space or something. How we want to serve our life ... the hero's adventure?" Come on, I found myself thinking. Come on, Truelove, you remember this.

He looked around the class for a long, dreadfully silent, second. "Has anyone been doing this assignment? Show of hands."

Nobody raised a hand. Not even me. I didn't think that one word, misery, counted.

"Yeah, that's what I thought." He walked to the front of the class, picked up a piece of chalk and slowly wrote, in capital letters, YOU WILL BE TESTED. The chalk broke. He turned around and looked at us. He walked to the back of the room. Nobody was breathing at this point, at least not loudly. At the door, he hurled the broken bit like a mini baseball. It hit the blackboard squarely with a soft ping. "Forget the assignment," he said. He opened the door and walked out. The bell rang.

It was silent for a full minute until Jumpy Kate spoke. "Which is it? We will be tested or we should forget the assignment? Am I missing something?"

Dell shook her head. "Yeah, you are."

Two days later we got a substitute teacher for the rest of the year. Ms. Johnson. Dell never paid up and I never asked.

• • •

"Jes, can we move our supper to tonight? Something's come up for tomorrow."

"Sure, Dad." It wasn't like this was the first time this had happened lately. I assumed it had something to do with the red-haired mother, but I wasn't asking any questions. "What's on the menu?"

"Grilled swordfish."

"Ooh, fancy."

"I am getting quite fancy."

"Don't get too fancy."

"I promise."

"When are you going to finish the room? It's not renovating itself."

There was no response.

"Hello?"

"Your mom ... well, she's not quite sure."

"Not quite sure about what?"

"Not sure if it's needed."

"Aha. So they *are* going to put the baby in a box beside the stove."

"What's that?"

"Nothing. Why isn't it needed?"

"Something about Angela moving in with her mother, possibly."

"Are you serious?"

"Listen, I'm not exactly in the know about what goes on over there." His tone was acidic.

"Okay, fine. Nobody tells me anything, but that's just fine."

"Dinner at six?"

"Fine."

• • •

I wandered over at about 6:15, a small rebellion. Why should I be Little Miss Punctual when everyone else was obviously just taking care of themselves? Besides, Moses was slowing me down. He seemed to have no self-restraint and was now the size of a small pig. "Must you smell every little piece of poo along the way?" I asked him. Now, *there* was a bit of life-affirming wisdom that I could live with. Forget about the roses, smell the poo.

I noticed a moving van outside the building, but thought nothing of it. Someone was always moving in or out. I had just reached the door when Mr. Truelove approached, carrying a large box. I darted behind the cement pillar, hoping the box was in his way and he hadn't seen me. The door opened and he walked straight to the truck. My stealth skills were obviously improving. Then he turned. "Hi, Jes. Hello, Moses."

Crap. "Oh, hi there, Mr. Truelove." I walked out from behind the pillar. "Good dog, Moses." I said. "He just had to ... you know."

Mr. Truelove nodded.

"So, you're moving?"

"Yep. Time to move on. Find new young minds to warp."

I didn't know what to say.

"Sorry. I shouldn't have said that."

"Oh, it's okay." I tried to slip over to the buzzer because the door had closed.

"Look, Jes. I'm sorry about the other day. I just lost it. Well, I guess that was obvious."

"Not really. Seriously, nobody noticed. It's public school, right? Last week Ms. Blanchard threw a student at the blackboard." I winced at yet another blurtation. I was unfixable.

But he laughed. Actually, he just smiled at first and then he laughed. A really nice, big laugh. So I laughed, too. What the heck.

"You're a good egg, Jes."

"Well, thanks."

"You are. You're smart and you're funny and you're very kind."

Oh, boy.

He moved toward the door with his keys. "Here, I'll let you in. Tell your dad hi for me, okay? I'll give him a call some time." He opened the door. "See you around."

The door started to close, but I couldn't let it. I held it open with my arm. "Um, Mr. Truelove?"

"Yeah?"

"I just wanted to say that I thought the assignment was a good one. I really did. It makes some sense to me."

"So you're going to do it?"

I flicked my hand. "Like Ms. Johnson would give us save-your ... er, extra marks for that. Phht. She's, trust me, a total tight ... um, she goes by the book. It's just that I like the part about the hero's adventure, that's all."

He smiled. "Well, good luck with that."

"Yeah, you, too."

"Hey, Jes, one final teaching moment."

"Okay." The guy did not know an exit line when it hit him in the face.

"Did you know that ninety-nine percent of humanity spends ninety-nine percent of their time trying to avoid painful truths?"

"What do they spend the other one percent doing?"

He smiled and pointed his finger at me the way he had on his drunken Christmas day. "See, now, *that's* a good question."

The door closed and I waved at him through the glass as he got into the van and drove away.

• • •

I decided to ask Angela, flat out, if she was moving in with her mother. I wasn't even quite sure why I wanted to know except, maybe, it would be nice to get things settled around here. Her moving wouldn't exactly qualify as a "painful truth," but at least it would be a truth and then I'd know. The baby was coming and, from the looks of my mother's bulging belly, soon. Somebody had to be organized.

I marched into her room. She was reading a book in the lotus position. I bent down. "Is it true?"

"Is what true?"

"Are you moving in with your mother?"

"Where did you hear that?"

"It doesn't matter where I get my information." I could be mysterious. "Are you moving?"

"Do you care?"

"Maybe. Sure. I don't know. Are you?"

"You want you room back, is that it?" She de-pretzeled herself and stood up.

"This is not about a room. This is about the truth. This is about that little moment ..."

Angela threw back her head and howled like a slightly crazed wolf. "Arrrrrgh. And I was so calm."

I decided not to say anything.

"Do you want to go shopping?" she asked suddenly.

"I hate shopping."

"No, you don't."

"Yes, I really do."

"You only think you hate shopping."

"There's a difference?"

"There's a total difference." Then she stopped. "Well, maybe there isn't. But the point is, you do it all wrong."

"There's a right way?"

"Yes, and I'm going to show you."

• • •

Two buses later, we were inside the mall. The last time we were here together we were arrested for shoplifting. Not really arrested — detained. I felt a little shiver of apprehension. Angela rolled her eyes at me as though she'd read my mind. "Don't worry, I've reformed."

"Yeah, that's what I thought while you scraped your key along Marshall's car."

She smiled at the memory. "I knew he'd never press charges."

She was right. My mother had been all set to do the right thing and "dialogue with his parents" until we dialogued her right out of that. Angela made the point that Marshall would never risk telling his parents about how or why it happened. I could tell that my mother's moral compass was spinning out of control over that one, but she'd reluctantly agreed. She told me later about how she was worried that Angela was a bad influence on me. Angela had overheard and then Cal walked in and it turned into a big almost-family conference/melee. Nothing was resolved and they were fighting in a most un-psychologist way when Angela and I left the room.

"Here's the thing," Angela said now. "You march into stores like a soldier who's sure he's going to die in the big battle before he even fires a shot."

"I march?"

"Yes, you do. Doomed. It's a self-fulfilling prophecy. You expect to be unsuccessful, so you are."

"So, what's the answer, Obi-Wan Kenobi?"

"Shoes."

"Shoes." What with the thrum of shopping noise and Muzak being pumped through the speakers like anthrax, I was fast falling into a coma. "Why shoes?"

"Because shoes are the only thing separating you from Mother Earth."

I followed her through the maze of shops. My own shoes were fast turning to cement.

"Also, they are the great equalizer. Everybody wears shoes."

"What if you have no legs?"

She sighed as we passed an Orange Julius stand. I looked longingly at it. "There you go, being all doomed again."

"Sorry."

"Okay."

She stopped suddenly at a shoe store, pivoted and was swallowed whole by the shop. I followed.

"Behold," she said with a sweep of her arm. "I give you shoes. Every shape and size to fit princess and commoner alike." Three guesses as to who I was. "High heels, low heels, open-toed, closed. Sandals, boots, pumps and runners. Leather, satin, canvas and" — she picked one up, inspected it and shuddered — "man-made materials. Bejeweled with ribbons, sequins and little puffy pom-poms." She moved farther into the darkest recesses of the store. "And here we have the land of the unwanted shoe. The sales rack. These are the hopeful shoes."

"Hmm, you see all that?"

She gazed at the rack. "Oh, much more. The trick is to find the pair that will make you the happiest."

"Shoes make you happy?"

"I said happiest, not happy. We're not talking a miracle here." She pulled out a high-heeled red shoe and showed it to me. "Now, this has potential. So we ask ourselves ... what would make this shoe the happiest?"

"But not happy," I said tiredly.

"Exactly!" She seemed encouraged, like I was a young Jedi who'd finally figured out what the light saber was for. "Now, focus. Jeans would work. These shoes would smile if you introduced them to a good pair of jeans. A little black dress would make them giddy. What about a short skirt?"

"Sure."

"No," she said abruptly. "You introduce these shoes to a short skirt and you know what they're going to say?" She waited.

"I don't know."

"They're going to say, 'Do I look like a hooker?'"

"Okay, you're officially nuts." I walked away as she continued to preach her doctrine of shoes. I don't think she noticed.

I was ambling (not marching) through the aisle of hopeful shoes when something winked at me from the bottom of the rack. I bent down to look closer. They were turquoise blue, the color Dell called tropical-island-where-I'll-live-one-day blue. They were low-heeled, like slippers, and covered with sequins. I picked one up. I took off my runner and slipped it on. It fit, ironically, like a glove.

Angela peeked around the corner and came toward me with a smirk. "By George, I think she's got it."

"Can I help you?" A sales clerk sidled up beside us. She looked bored, like she didn't realize she was working in a haven of endless possibility.

"Do you have these in a size seven?" I asked.

The girl shrugged. "Probably not. It's the sales rack."

"Could you check?"

"I suppose." She took the other shoe with her and wandered away.

"And you think my attitude is bad," I said to Angela, who was kneeling in front of me. "What are you doing?" She had her hand pressed on the toe of the shoe.

"But this shoe fits perfectly." She looked up with genuine concern on her face.

The perky clerk returned with a box in her hand. "Wow, you are so lucky."

I took the box from her and gave back the shoe I'd been wearing. "Thanks."

Angela followed me to the cashier. "You should never buy shoes that are too small, Jes. I understand the impulse, honestly, I do. But seriously, you'll be sorry."

"Relax, Angela. I've figured out what would make these shoes the happiest. You should be thrilled."

"What?" she asked as I pulled out my wallet.

"Dell."

• • •

After that, Angela had some "serious" shopping to do. I found myself a smoothie and a bench under a fake palm tree. Every once in a while I peeked inside the box and had a nice warm feeling when I thought about giving the shoes to Dell. The Muzak had almost lulled me to sleep when Angela returned, arms full of bags. She was wearing new sunglasses. She looked like a movie star, I'd give her that. Or an actor, whatever.

"What's in the little one?" I asked.

"Nothing."

"Wow. You ran out of things to buy so they gave you a bag for the nothing. That's very Nirvana, isn't it?"

She smiled. "You're occasionally funny."

"Seriously, what's in the bag?"

"Seriously, why do you care?"

I groaned and snatched the bag. This caused the others to fall, so I had some time while she gathered. I peeked inside the folds of tissue. A powder-blue swath of fabric peeked back. I pulled it out. It was a sleeper. A tiny little sleeper that looked like it would fit a doll. It was so soft that I held it up to my cheek. "Oh, man, this is incredible." Then I looked at the price tag. "Fifty bucks!"

"It's Dolce and Gabbana."

"It's who and what?"

"A designer."

Outside, the bus had just pulled up. We hurried over, boarded and found seats. Angela took the sleeper back and folded it carefully inside the tissue.

"Man, what a scam," I said. "But it is soft, I'll give you that."

"A baby's first experience with fabric should be a sensual one."

"But my mom isn't due for another four weeks!"

Angela shrugged.

I looked out the window and watched the scenery float past. "You're not sticking around, are you?"

Chapter Twenty

Mom was sitting in the living room when we got home, Moses curled at her feet. I did a quick mental check to see if I'd done anything wrong and found my conscience clear. "Hey, Mom."

Angela walked past us to the stairs.

"Did you have a nice time shopping?" Mom asked, but she looked distracted.

"Are you okay?" Angela asked.

"Oh, just a few Braxton Hicks."

My baby homework had fallen sadly by the wayside. "Is that a designer?" I asked. Nobody smiled.

"They're fake contractions," Angela explained. "Are you sure? How far apart are they?"

"I think I know Braxton Hicks, Angela. This isn't my first time." She smiled, but it was a Bernadette smile.

"Okay, I'll be in my room," Angela said.

"Well, that was friendly," I said after her door closed.

Mom closed her eyes. "I know. I'll apologize later. It's just that she knows everything. And I'm tired." She opened her eyes again. "I feel like Moby Dick."

"You should have a nap. I'll get dinner started."

"Not that kind of tired, Jes." She rubbed her shoulder with her hand. "Everything aches. Every single part of me. What was I thinking, to do this at my age?"

"You're not so ancient."

"Oh, I am. I am."

"Do you want some ice cream and a pickle? We won't tell Angela. It'll be our little secret."

She took my hand suddenly. "Jes, it isn't working."

"What's not working?"

"This. Us. Cal and I are fighting all the time ..."

I took my hand away. A sharp arrow of fear plunged into my gut. "Oh, no. This isn't another ice-cream situation, is it?"

"What?"

"Remember — when you told me about you and dad. How the ice cream melts, leaving just the gooey topping. How you try and try but you can't ..."

"I don't remember that, but, no, this isn't a melting marriage."

"Then what is it?"

"Listen to me. And take that stricken look off your face, please. Cal and I just feel that it might be better if Angela lived with her mother."

"Better for who?"

"Better for all of us. Cal and Angela don't really have a relationship. She was just a baby when he and Bernadette split up and — "

"When he left."

"You don't know the whole story there."

"Of course I don't. It's not like somebody ever told me, is it?"

"I didn't ... you're right. Okay ..." She put her hands across her belly. A look of pain crossed her face. I could actually see her belly stiffen and then the whole thing shifted like, well, a tectonic shift.

"Whoa," I sat. "What was that?"

She leaned with her eyes closed, not hearing me. Then she opened them again. "He's getting restless," she smiled. She rubbed her hands across her stomach like she was soothing him. I suddenly felt a pang for another time and another baby. I pushed the thought away.

"Do you remember the New Year's party we went to at Bernadette's?"

I nodded, trying to catch up to the conversation.

"Well, she got a little drunk. She told Cal that he wasn't Angela's father."

Okay, I was caught up. "What?"

She shook her head. "It's not like he didn't suspect. There were ... circumstances. But this made it official."

"Why would she lie to him about something like that?"

She smiled again, this time like she was talking to a moron. "So he'd marry her, of course. He has tried, Jes, he really has. But there's so much going on now and it's just not working. Second marriages are difficult.

Blended families are difficult. At the best of times."

"And these are the worst of times?"

"I'm not sure how they could get much worse. Cal and I can't agree on anything about how to handle the two of you."

"Handle us!"

She put her hand out, but I pushed it away.

"I didn't mean that. Or maybe I did, I don't know. I don't know what I'm doing, that's the truth of it. There. I have no idea what I'm doing. I think the best thing would be if Angela was with her mother."

"With the drunken, lying, evil Botox queen?"

"Jes!"

"Mom!" I stood up.

"Stay here and talk to me."

"Angela can't stand her."

"She's talked to you about it?"

"Yes. No. Not really, just once. But can't you see it? Who sits around in their room and meditates all day?" I stopped, suddenly sick of being the one who had to figure things out. "Never mind. Whatever." I left the room. She didn't try to stop me. Didn't even try to "talk things out." I looked at her through the slats in the banister. My Therapist Mom had disappeared somewhere inside that big, pregnant lady.

Upstairs, I passed Angela in the hallway. I wondered if she'd heard. I was horrified at the thought.

She smiled. "Don't worry about it. I knew. Cal told me the other day. It's not a big deal. Seriously."

• • •

Dell met me at the park. I took the shoes and Moses. The shoes seemed like a ridiculous idea now, but they didn't fit me. And if the shoe doesn't fit ... send it to live with its mother. Something like that.

Dell was sitting on a swing. I tied Moses's leash to a tree.

"No, give him to me." She held out her hands.

"He's as big as a pig."

"Shh. He is not." She went over and hoisted him up in her arms. I could tell right away that she knew it was a bad idea. But she lugged him over anyway.

We sat there for a while, not saying anything, just swinging aimlessly. What was the point of swings again? How come they used to be so much fun? The park was barren and the trees looked naked. Tiny buds covered their spindly arms like goose bumps.

I told Dell about Angela and Cal and the big plan. She didn't respond at first. Then she said, "Maybe it's for the best."

Maybe it was. Maybe that's what the real best was, kind of crappy most of the time.

"What's in the bag?" she asked.

"Nothing much."

"Well, that's weird." She dragged her feet in the dirt. "What's in the bag?"

I handed it to her. "It's for you."

"No. Really?"

"Yes, really. I was shopping."

"You were shopping?"

"Just open it."

Unceremoniously, she dumped Moses off her lap, then apologized. He seemed happy to be free to root around, looking for truffles probably. "Oh!" she squealed. She sounded like the old Dell. "They're beautiful. They're for me?"

"Well, they don't fit me. I have the feet of a commoner."

She held them up, put one on each hand and pretended to walk them around in the air. "They're so pretty. You bought them for me? Why did you do that?"

I laughed. "This is not a national event."

"It should be ... National Shoe Day," she said, but she was busily taking off her boots and replacing them with the sparkly shoes. They looked nice on her feet, even with the argyle socks. "They are perfect. Thank you, Jes. They'll look great with jeans, don't you think?"

"I do. I really do. I think that jeans will make those shoes absolutely giddy with happiness." I swung faster.

She ignored me, enveloped in the act of admiring her shoes, walking back and forth in front of the swings. I could feel the wind now and the smell of almost-spring. I could feel the smell; that was weird. Through the tangled branches I could see the roof of my house and Sam's.

"But why, Jes? Seriously, why?"

I slowed down and let my feet drag me to a stop. My heart was beating fast from the exertion. "They reminded me of those shoes that Dorothy wore in *The Wizard of Oz*, except blue."

She thought about this. Then she stood still and tapped them together. "So I can go home whenever I want."

"Something like that."

"Back to Kansas."

"Yep."

She looked at me and her eyes were sparkly, like the shoes. "I love them."

I hadn't seen her eyes like that since the awful day. "Are you okay?" I asked suddenly.

"I will be." She sat back down and began to swing. "Oh, I have news for you."

"What?"'

"Marshall and I are back together."

I lurched to a complete stop and twisted the chain of the swing so that I could look at her completely. "You're what?"

She grinned like a lunatic and swung faster. "You. Are. So." She pumped her legs until she was framed against the empty branches. "Gullible. What am I going to do with you?"

She laughed hysterically. Then she let go and flew through the air, legs first. She landed neatly and spun around, still laughing.

She stopped laughing. "Oh, no. My shoes. My

beautiful shoes." She hobbled back to the swing and sat down. She removed one and rubbed at it fiercely. "I got dirt on them."

"Just a little bit," I said. "They'll survive."

"Yeah," she said. But she continued to clean it until most of the dirt was gone. She placed the shoes carefully in the bag and put her boots back on. "You're hopeless, you know."

"I do know that. Why, again?"

"You're hopelessly optimistic."

"Me?"

"Yep."

"You've got the wrong girl. That's you."

She shook her head. "No, not anymore. And, anyway, I wasn't optimistic, Jes. I was hopelessly oblivious, and I'm not anymore. It's a bad way to live. But you, you just keep trying to fix things. You believe."

"I don't know."

"Remember when we used to act out all the fairy tales? I was always the princess and you were always the witch or the wolf or the evil stepmother."

"Was I? I was never the princess?"

"Nope."

"Well, that was mean."

"Yep. But you always played along and you always believed in happily ever after."

"That was stupid."

"I don't think so. Believing in something isn't the same as making it up."

I hesitated, but then I couldn't stop myself. Cuz I'm a blurter. "But you believed in you and Marshall."

She nodded. "And that was wrong. But I don't think it's wrong to believe in love. It would be wrong not to, to give up — that's what I think now. And that's what you never did."

I looked toward the trees, but I couldn't see Sam's house. "I think you're wrong about that."

"No, you're just scared. And that's the thing. I was never scared. Never. I just thought things would work out. They don't always work out. And you know what else?"

"What else?"

"It's just stupid to go down with the ship, that's what I figure. If the stupid captain wants to, fine. But I say swim. That's what I say. *Hasta la vista*, baby, you were a good ship, but now you're sinking and I'm swimming to shore."

"I like this non-oblivious you."

"Yeah, well, get used to her, baby. Go."

"Huh?"

"Go to your man."

"I haven't got a man."

"Yes, you do."

I sat there.

"Why are you not going? That was your big moment to go sprinting through the woods." She looked disgruntled.

"It's just that ..."

"You're scared. I know. That's okay."

"I am scared, but that's not it. It's ... I'm really tired of losing people." Suddenly tears were dripping down my face even though I didn't even feel like I was crying. It was a waterfall of sadness coming from somewhere I couldn't see.

Dell got off the swing and kneeled in the dirt in front of me. She held onto my knees while I cried.

"When you were in that house," I finally said, "on that bed, I was paralyzed. I couldn't stand it if something happened to you, but Angela was the one who figured it out and got us to the party. She helped you. She knew what to do. I felt so helpless. It wasn't just you. It was my little sister and my parents and everything. I thought I'd already done this. I thought it had all gone away. But I don't think it ever goes away and I can't just keep handling it." I wiped the tears off my face. "I don't think I'm a very good handler."

"I know," she said. And she did, in her way. "But you don't have to handle everything. That's where you're stupid."

I sniffed.

"You're pretty smart, you're just not real smart. Sam is Sam."

"But what if it doesn't work out? I can't lose anyone else."

She shrugged. "If it doesn't work, it doesn't. Then

you'll handle that because you are fairly good at it and I'll help you and you won't be alone. Sam is Sam, but love is love. It doesn't go away."

"What does that mean?"

"Nobody ever gives up on love. Nobody ever does, they just pretend. Sometimes it's in broken pieces all over the ground, but that doesn't mean it's not there." She stopped to take a breath.

I wiped my entire face with the sleeve of her jacket. "Now you're hopeless."

"I am a hopeless realist. Now go."

I stood up shakily. "Sam is Sam, right?"

She threw her hands up over her head. "Sam couldn't be any more Sammier."

"Could you take Moses home?"

She nodded. She waved her arm like a wand. "Off with you. To your man."

As I left the park, I heard her call after me. "And thanks for the snot on my jacket."

"No problem," I yelled back.

Chapter Twenty-One

I didn't sprint to Sam's house. I walked slowly, practically ambled. I felt naked without Moses, and naked about doing what I seemed to be doing. When I reached his house I ambled right past. At my driveway I turned around, walked back to Sam's house and stood in his driveway. Then I walked back to mine. Then I walked back to Sam's. This went on for quite a while.

Somewhere, mid-amble, Henry appeared. "What are you doing?"

"I'm ... nothing. Is Sam home?"

"Why, do you want to kiss him?" He made a smooching noise. I glared at him. Henry glared back.

"Yes," I finally said. "I want to kiss him. What are you going to do about it?"

He seemed a little surprised at this. "He's in the darkroom."

"Fine."

I knocked on the door and, when Amber answered, I didn't even say hello. "I would like to kiss your son," I said. "Is that okay with you?"

She waved me past with her cup of coffee. "He's in the darkroom."

"Fine."

I walked straight in and almost lost my nerve. He was hanging up photos of our bleak winter. Sam is Sam, I reminded myself. Sam is Sam.

"Hey," he said.

"I would like to kiss you. Do you have a problem with that?"

"Uh, no."

"Okay, then." I stood rooted to the ground. And totally lost my nerve.

He tipped his head to the side. "You mean, like, now, or just generally?"

"Just generally."

"Okay." He continued to hang up pictures. "Because we could do it now, if you wanted."

"I know," I said. Suddenly I felt like taking a swing at something. That didn't seem normal. But what did I know about kissing? Nothing. "What about that black-haired party girl, huh? What about her?"

He ducked under the clothesline and stood in front of me. "She's got brown hair. She dyes it."

I nodded. "Well, it suits her. Does she make you happy?" I could smell the shampoo in his hair that he probably just washed because it was wet and he must have known it would make me stupid.

"I met her at the party and I haven't seen her since."

"The party that you asked me to?"

"I didn't ask you and, besides, you said no."

"I said no to something you didn't ask me to? That makes sense." I started backing up to the door, holding up my hands in surrender. Sam followed. When I reached the door, I stopped, because that's what closed doors will do to you.

"Last time I kissed you was in elementary school and you got really, really mad," he said.

"That's ... that is a true recollection. This is dangerous."

He smiled. Then he leaned forward and kissed me softly on the lips. When he moved his head away, I put my hand behind his damp neck and I kissed him. I felt the smoothness of his teeth with my tongue and tasted toothpaste. But the best thing, or at least the second best, was that the whole time I was kissing him I was thinking, *I can't wait to tell Sam.*

And then I heard Amber in the hallway calling my name. Sam moved back. He ran his hand through his hair; so cute, he made my heart bend.

"Jessica?" she said again. She opened the door. "That was your dad. Your mother's gone to the hospital. Your dad is on his way to take you."

• • •

"Is she okay?" I asked my dad as we sped to the hospital.

"I think so. I don't know."

"But isn't this early? Will the baby be okay?"

"I hope so."

"You hope so? That's your idea of reassuring me?"

"I don't know, Jes. I'm not part of this."

His words landed with a clunk on hard earth. Back to its normal rotation.

Cal was there when we arrived. I rushed to him. "What's going on? Is the baby okay? Is Mom okay?"

"She's seven centimeters dilated. The head is engaged."

"Engaged? Engaged in what? Mortal combat? To be married?" I looked for someone to speak English to me.

Angela stepped forward. "Everything is progressing normally."

"Why didn't you just say that?" I asked Cal in a really attractive, shrill voice. "Can I see her?"

He nodded. "I'll take you."

We moved quickly through the softly lit hallway. Why wasn't it brighter? How could anyone see what was going on? We entered another softly lit room and I thought everyone must have lost their minds. Music was playing and the room was painted a delicate mauve. Where were the bright lights, the instruments, the drugs? I needed drugs.

I rushed over to the bed. Mom was smiling, and this surprised me. "Are you okay?"

"I'm fine, Sweetie." Then, just like that, her face twisted. "Oh, boy, here we go." And then she looked terrified.

Cal took her hand. He stared right into her eyes and she stared back. I moved away. She breathed, in and out, softly at first and then panting. "Slow down," he said. "That's right. That's right. You're good, you're doing great. You are doing everything just right." His voice was completely calm, completely unfreaked out. I watched my mother's eyes on his, unblinking, like there was some kind of force field pulling them together. And then it was over and she closed her eyes. Cal buried his head in her hair and gently stroked her stomach. My eyes filled with tears. He murmured something and she touched his shorn head, murmured back.

I backed over to the door and saw my father. "I'll just get going," he said.

Oh, God, I thought, he saw everything. "I'm sorry," I whispered.

Mom said, "Thanks for bringing her."

I held Dad's hand as we walked to the elevator. He pressed the button, leaned over and hugged me. "This is good, Pumpkin. Don't worry about me, okay?" He put his hand under my chin. "Really, I mean it. I'm fine."

"Don't go," I said.

"I really should. I don't belong here."

"I need you."

"You'll be fine."

"No. I need you. I can't handle this, Dad. There is

going to be blood and guts and placenta. I read about it. Do you have any idea how this works? The birth canal spreads." I held out my hands from an inch to about a foot. "And then a huge head comes flying through like a bowling ball. And then there's the pushing and heaving and bleeding ..."

"Okay, okay," he said. The elevator opened and closed again. "I'll stay. Let's see if we can get you an epidural."

"That's all I'm saying!"

• • •

We went down to the cafeteria for coffee. When we got back, the waiting room was full of familiar faces. Sam was there with Amber and Geoff and Danny. (Henry was probably robbing a liquor store.) Dell and her mother sat with them. Angela was in a corner with Bernadette — Bernice, as I liked to think of her. What was she doing here?

I didn't know where to go first. I waved to them all, but I was overwhelmed with how not alone I was. Dell rushed over.

"Sam said he kissed you."

"He did? He told you!"

"Blurted it out before I could even ask, which I was totally going to do. You guys are so perfect."

"Perfect?"

"In a completely realistic way."

I was about to go over to Sam when I noticed Bernadette stand and leave the room. I looked at Dell, who shrugged. Then Angela disappeared. "I'll be right back," I said. "Tell Sam to keep his big trap shut."

I followed Angela into a stairwell, down a flight of stairs, to the floor below. I wondered if she was trying to find a place to meditate. Personally, I felt it was a time to medicate. She finally stopped in front of a big window. When I caught up, I saw a row of perfectly spaced basinets, holding perfectly blanketed newborns.

We stood side by side. If she was surprised that I was there she didn't show it. Finally I said, "Your mother left."

"Yeah."

"What's up with that?"

"She's moving back to California. More opportunities there, you know. She's still looking for her big break."

"I thought she liked it here."

"Yeah, well, small pond, right? She wants me to come with her. She sees big things for us ... for me. Although that's the same thing to her." She spread her hands on the window. "They're so cute, aren't they? So new."

I shook my head. "So you told her that you're not her meal ticket, right? That's why she left?"

Angela turned her head slowly. "Oh, no. I'm going. I just didn't want her sticking around. She doesn't belong here." She took her hands away from the window. "*I* don't belong here."

"Yes, you do." I was going to launch into a big speech about the whole blender/smoothie theory of life when she held up a hand.

"Don't."

"Don't what?"

"This is the canoe moment."

"The what?"

"Last summer when you gave me the touching monologue about how life wasn't a fairy tale and ... and then we fell into the water and you jumped off the rope swing for the first time and it was this big moment."

"Well ..."

"I gave it a shot, Jes. But I don't belong here. Cal is not my father. He's just some hapless guy who tried to love me."

The hallway fell silent except for the muffled cry of a baby. We watched as a burly nurse picked it up and held it to his chest.

"Have you seen Cal with your mother, Jes?"

I nodded.

"No, really, have you seen it?"

"Yeah, I saw it."

"He's not a bad guy. In fact, he's a good guy. And his baby deserves a real shot. Their baby." She saw my face. "You have a waiting room full of people who love you. You're this little whacked-out person who everybody loves." She reached into her purse and pulled out a beautifully wrapped package. "Give this to them, okay?"

"You give it to them."

"No, my mom's waiting in the car. She was so pleased about being told what to do, let me tell you."

"You have to wait until the baby is born. He's your brother!" I wanted to take the words back the minute they were out.

"No," she shook her head. "He's not."

"Okay, so you're just going to leave without saying good-bye?"

"Good-byes are overrated."

This is what I'd thought I wanted once upon a time. I hadn't asked to have her in my life, hadn't really wanted her there. But now she was going and it seemed wrong. "Okay, so not good-bye?"

She just stood there.

"See — sometimes that's what good-byes are for," I said helpfully. I was going for a joke, but I couldn't have been more wrong. Her eyes were wet.

"Angela ..."

She turned to me abruptly. "Can I tell you something? I've only told one other person."

"Okay."

"Remember when I told you that I didn't have to go to the hospital?"

I struggled to remember.

"The night that Marshall ... and Dell ..."

Our night of vandalism. "Yeah, of course."

"I didn't."

"Um ... confused here."

"But I should have. I should have gone to the hospital. I was pretty messed up. The same thing happened to me that would have happened to Dell. Except it was my mother's boyfriend."

"Oh my God."

"Yeah. Um, it was bad. I was, like, fourteen." She wiped a tear away. "They're so sweet, aren't they?" she said, pointing to the babies. "So innocent."

"You said you told someone," I blurted out.

"Yeah," she shrugged. "My mom. She said it was probably a misunderstanding."

"What?" I could picture the horde of social workers, policemen and SWAT teams my mother would have assembled if something like that happened to me. "She said it was a *what*?"

Angela turned to me. "Not the point, Jes. So not the point. My mother is my mother. She will never change. I'm not telling you so that you'll get mad at her."

"Why are you telling me?"

"Because, if I had hung around, I could teach him." She pointed to the row of babies. "Not that every guy is like that, I know. But I just wanted to tell him that when some stupid little girl who's dressed up like a tart because she thinks it makes her look pretty says yes, sometimes it means maybe. And sometimes it turns into a no. And it's the no that counts. It's the no that he has to pay attention to."

"I am so sorry."

"Well, me, too. Now you'll have to tell him."

"You can't go back with her."

"I don't have a choice. I don't belong here. You're not my family. I'm stronger now, Jes, honestly."

Arguments swirled around in my brain, not least of which was the problem that she presented: Was she family? And then Dell came racing down the hallway, slipping in her blue shoes. She practically bounced off the walls. A nurse shh-ed her, but she kept barreling, like a baby out of the birth canal. "She's pushing," she finally said, panting as though she was the one in labor. "The baby is coming."

"Already?"

"It's not uncommon with a second pregnancy," said Angela, back to her all-knowing self.

"Third," I corrected automatically.

"What?"

I waved my hand. "No time now. I have to go. We have to go. You can't leave until the baby is born. Promise me."

Angela hesitated.

"Promise me."

"Promise her," Dell glowered, suddenly my knight in shining armor. She looked over at me as if to say, Why am I saying this?, but she just repeated the words. "You promise her right now or ..."

"Or what?" Angela said, crossing her arms in front of her.

"Or else."

Angela rolled her eyes.

I watched them square off and sighed. "Or you could thank her for saving your ass at the New Year's party."

Dell shrugged. "Or I could do that."

"Way to go, Dell," I shouted as I sprinted away.

• • •

When I arrived, the room went fuzzy and I had to sit down. Nobody noticed. They were busy. The lights were finally on. The doctor was leaning in and I couldn't see anything because of the tent-like sheet pitched around Mom's hips. Cal breathed along with my mother, in perfect, panting harmony. There was groaning, and heaving ... just like the books said. The door opened quietly. "Get over here, Angela," I hissed.

"Shh," she said.

I heard the doctor tell my mother to push. She gave such a mighty heave that I thought her head was going to explode. The sound was unearthly. I grabbed Angela's hand and she didn't let go.

The doctor pulled. That wasn't right, was it? This was a baby, not taffy. But nobody else seemed alarmed. My mother gave one final groan and heave and the doctor smiled, holding something very goopy. "Well, hello there, little one," she said.

I expelled a huge breath of pent-up air and I moved fast. I peeked over the doctor's shoulders as she mopped off the blood and guts, and then I gasped.

"Where's the penis?"

Chapter Twenty-Two

The doctor smiled. "She doesn't need one."

While everyone laughed in delight, I volunteered to tell the waiting-room people that the baby had arrived. She was here. She.

I told the story in such vivid color and detail that Danny looked like he was going to puke. Amber took him outside. Then, in front of everyone, Sam kissed me. And the weird thing — the nice thing — was that I didn't even feel like slugging him. Not one bit.

"That was nice," I said.

"It really was," Sam agreed. "I think we could be good at this."

"Oh, brother," Dell said. Then she led him away and I could hear her explaining how this wasn't going to change the friendship between the three of us, not in the slightest, and here were the rules ... As her voice drifted away, I realized that everyone had left except for my dad.

I walked with him to his car.

"A girl," he said in the elevator.

"I know," I said. "Yes."

• • •

In the parking lot we looked for his car. It was where we'd left it, of course, but things had changed since then. The earth had done another tectonic shift.

"So," he said, "you're okay now?"

"It's a gruesome process."

"But look at the outcome." He kissed the top of my head.

"I'm sorry, Dad."

"Why?"

"I didn't think about you at all. I mean, I did. But I needed you, so I didn't care."

He hugged me tightly. "And that was great."

"What?"

"It's great to be needed, kiddo. Sometimes I wonder how I fit into your life anymore."

"But you're my dad."

He hugged me again. And when he pulled away, he didn't have that broken-guy look on his face. He got into the car. "It's what I'm most proud of."

"Well," I said. "You need to get out more."

"I think we're going to have to hire someone to finish that wall off, okay?"

"Yeah."

"You understand?"

"I do. So how's it going with that lady, Billi?"

"Pretty good. Not bad."

"Yeah, well, I've been meaning to tell you, that Marmalade ... she's delightful."

He laughed. "Right. She wants us to call her Mandy now."

I smiled.

"You and Sam, hmm?"

"Yeah."

He sighed and started the engine. "Just let me know if I need to beat him up or anything, okay?"

"I'll do that." I closed the door and waved him away.

• • •

The baby had been cleaned up and bundled into a beige blanket with a pink cap tucked around her perfect head. She looked like a little mini rap artist. I arrived just as a nurse was taking her to the nursery below so that "Mum" could rest.

"What do you think?" asked Cal, beaming. I'd never seen him beam before.

"She's perfect," I said. I remembered something. I grabbed the package from beside my chair and handed it to my mom. "This is from Angela."

"Both of us," Angela said quickly.

"No," I glared. "I would have bought overalls and I never would have spent that much money."

My mother held up the ridiculously over-priced sleeper. "Oh, it's beautiful."

"I'm sorry that it's blue," Angela said.

I saw the look that passed across my mother's face.

"But you know," said Angela, "she can pull it off,

I think. Not all girls can. It matches her eyes, although that could change. You don't know right away with eye color."

My mother smiled at me. "That's true," she said.

"Listen, I should get going. My mom's waiting."

Cal and Mom nodded.

Wait a minute. "Did you know that she's leaving?" I asked.

"She just said that she was leaving," Cal explained, thus cementing the fact that he was my mother's match at declaring the obvious.

"No. Leaving leaving. Leaving for California."

"I left a note. It's better this way." Angela picked up her purse.

Cal blurted. "But I bought you a bike." Who knew he was a blurter?

"You bought me a bike?"

"I know we talked about you living with your mother, but I thought that meant here. I thought we could ride together, get to know each other."

Angela didn't seem to know what to do with this. But she was blinking pretty darn fast. "You bought me a bike," she repeated.

Now Cal seemed at a loss for words.

I wasn't. Especially as the silence grew. "Did you buy *me* a bike?"

Cal looked alarmed. "Um, no. I'm sorry. I was just thinking that ..."

"I'm kidding, Cal."

He scraped a hand across his head. "Sometimes I don't get your sense of humor."

"Me, neither." Angela sniffed.

"I know," added my mother.

"Sheesh," I said, walking toward the door. "You are a stern, humorless people. You guys figure this out, okay? I'm going to see how my little unnamed sibling is doing. And, Angela, maybe you want to consider who is going to help her accessorize if you're not around."

She stopped me at the door. "She has an outfit with rhinestone buttons. What kind of earrings does she wear?"

I thought. "Sparkly ones?"

She sighed. "Is she in line to be the Queen of England?"

• • •

I walked downstairs to the big window. The lights were low. I saw a reflection I'd been avoiding. "Hey there," I said. "You look like me. Have you ever wanted to give a speech about how life is full of the unexpected and how maybe that's good? How it's not okay just to smell the poo, how there's more? That it's a hero's adventure, even if it's only one percent of the time?"

A nurse came up beside me. "Do you want me to turn the lights up? So you're not just talking to yourself?" She reached her hand around the wall and the room brightened. "Which one's yours?"

I pointed to the little cutie in the pink cap.

"Oh! You're the girl who shouted, 'Where's the penis?'"

See — that's what you get remembered for. Life is so not fair.

• • •

When I returned to my mother's room, Angela and Cal were heading to the elevator.

"I'm giving Angela a ride home. Your mom's resting. I just need to ask the nurse about something. I'll be right back." He walked to the nurse's station.

"So you're staying?" I asked Angela.

She shrugged. "For now."

The smoothie speech presented itself in my mind. How some of us were strawberries and blueberries and kiwi, but other people were the milk, yogurt and ice cream — making things smoother. And, of course, there were the nuts and the pieces of toffee that never completely emulsified, but added a little surprise every once in a while.

"As opposed to the Eternal Now?" I said instead.

She smiled.

"Now is good," I said.

"Your mom told me about Alberta."

I nodded.

"I'm sorry."

"Yeah."

Her eyes glimmered with tears, but she blinked them back. "She asked me to be godmother."

I smiled. Nicely done, Mom. "Her fairy godmother? That's perfect."

But Angela shook her head. "No, thanks. Just real life."

"No glass slippers?"

She hesitated. "Maybe."

"So what does a regular godmother do?"

"Spiritual guidance, obviously. And personal-style advice."

"Sounds good, sounds real."

"You guys might be annoying at times, but you're good at real."

"You're not so bad at it yourself."

"Yeah, well," she shrugged. As she turned to leave, she glanced at her reflection in the hall mirror. "Jeez, I look terrible."

"You really do."

She scowled. Then she smiled wickedly. "Where's the penis? That was a great moment."

"Whatever."

"Let's go, girls," Cal called from the elevator.

"I'll come later," I said. "I'll take a bus."

"Are you sure?" he asked.

"Well, if I had a bike ..."

Cal looked disconcerted; Angela rolled her eyes. The elevator door closed.

Chapter Twenty-Three

I crept into the room. One light burned dimly above my mother's head. Her eyes were closed. I pulled up the chair, perched my feet on the iron rungs of the bed. I breathed the antiseptic air.

"What are we going to do, Jes?"

"Huh?"

Mom opened her eyes. "I don't have a name for her. Christopher, Dylan, Matthew, Brian ..."

"I like Brian," I said.

She smiled and then it flickered. Her mouth tightened. Her whole face was fighting the inevitable but tired of crying. Or of trying not to. "What are we going to do?" she said again.

There was a soft knock at the door and a jolly nurse walked in. She rolled the basinet over to my mother. "I'm sorry for coming back so soon, but somebody's hungry."

As my mother took the blanketed bundle from her, I thought to myself, That's my sister. Then I corrected myself: that's my half-sister. Then I corrected my correction: half of what? DNA? Genetic code? Blood? It was stupid. She was a total whole: fingers, toes, torso, little fuzzy head. Totally new.

I watched as my mother guided this newly born whole person to her breast. Watched as this newly born latched on and sucked. The nurse clucked approvingly and left the room.

"She knows what to do," said my mother. "Look at her, Jes."

I nodded.

"You didn't have a clue. You screeched like an owl."

I rolled my eyes. "I must have missed that class."

"So did Alberta. It took her two whole days. I thought I was going to have to bottle-feed her. She had strong opinions." She looked up at me with shimmering eyes. "I miss her."

"Me, too." And I knew right then that we always would. It would never change and it was all right. In fact, it was right.

"Here," she said, lifting the tiny bundle to me. "She needs to burp."

I hesitated. Tiny bundle, tiny moment that seemed to hold everything. I took it in my arms. You have to be a total idiot not to know, instinctively, how to hold a baby.

"Rub her gently," Mom instructed.

"Just when I was ready to beat her senseless," I said, rubbing gently. I stroked her tiny little self until there was an expulsion of air. I felt triumphant. "Atta girl," I said. Blue eyes that might change peered up at me, unblinking, full of trust. "I think Dad's going to be okay," I said.

"He told you that he's off the job?"

"Yeah. He's moving on."

"I think he is." She dabbed her eyes with the end of her blanket. "It was good to have him there, though, to tear down the old wall. We'll have to rebuild it ourselves. Is that okay?"

I smiled at her. Good old Metaphor Mom. "Nice to have you back," I said. It was a good moment until I noticed something warm and gooey in my hand. "Oh, man," I howled. "She pooped on me. Oh, gross." I looked into her eyes and I was pretty sure she winked. "You little poopster."

"We're not calling her Poopster."

I handed her to my mother, who seemed to know what to do.

• • •

Once upon a time there was a family. It changed. Then there was a new family. And it changed. The princess was dismayed, disappointed and disillusioned. And a little fed up. This was not how she pictured her life. (She also thought she would be taller.) Then, one day, out of nowhere, she had a thought. It came not in a dream, but a recipe: Take a family, add a beautiful, criminally savvy stepsister, a wicked step-something, a balding, biking man and a baby with either incredibly bad timing or an incredibly good sense of humor. Throw in a dad who could easily show up with a new wife and two red-headed brats — I wouldn't put it past him. Toss in hope, humor and love — a ridiculous amount of love. And blend.

Also by Gayle Friesen

Losing Forever

With themes such as coping with change, dealing with divorce and falling in love, this novel speaks to young adults in a realistic, unsentimental voice. *Losing Forever* introduces Jes and her friends and family, whom readers meet again in *For Now*.

"... spirited dialogue and well-developed characters."
— *School Library Journal*

"Friesen convincingly and respectfully handles Jes's anxiety as she negotiates these not-so-everyday trials." — *Horn Book Guide*

The Isabel Factor

"... particularly well-crafted novel which conveys a worthwhile message: 'just be yourself.'" — *Booklist*

Men of Stone

"... very well-written ... fully realized, funny and charming character." — *Kirkus Reviews*

Janey's Girl

"A stunning debut. The main characters are real — interesting and imperfect." — *Quill & Quire*

Awards and honors for Gayle Friesen's novels:

Junior Library Guild selection

American Library Association Best Books for Young Adults selection

Society of School Librarians International Honor Book

Governor General's Award finalist

Canadian Library Association Young Adult Canadian Book Award

The New York Public Library Books for the Teen Age list

Red Maple Book Award